DRAGO BONEZ: ORIGINS
PART ONE

Co-Author **Chelsi R. Hargrove**

Editor **Talia Servi**

This is a work of fiction. Names, characters, places, and incidents either are the product of the author's imagination or are used fictitiously. Any resemblance to actual persons, living or dead, events, or locales is entirely coincidental.

Copyright © 2021 by Drago Bonez: Origins Part One, its author Jeremy B. Pereyra, and associated affiliates.

All rights reserved. No part of this book may be reproduced or used in any manner without written permission of the copyright owner except for the use of quotations in a book review. For more information, address: DragoBonez@gmail.com.

First Revised Edition AUGUST 2021

DEDICATION

To those we have lost, to those we have loved. To those still here who carry our love. To those we are surrounded with, and those distanced apart. To those who will always remain within our hearts.

CHAPTER ONE
This is My Story

This battle was like no other I have faced in the past. The stench of war fumed around us in the whiplashing winds. The pools of blood that had been spilt on this day began to puddle in the footprints of battle. Clashing of steel and agonizing cries of pain echoed through the battlegrounds. We were living within an everlasting song of death that seemed to never silence.

Through the thickened fog of war, my eyes still bore witness to the bloodied canvas in which these once peaceful lands have become. Nydeli herself has become cracked and shattered throughout her entirety. The mass of this ever-going war brought upon havoc in lands that had been serene for many generations. In the trail of this enemy, our world has become forever stained with the lives of those who have fought and are still fighting.

The enemy we face has become this world's greatest threat. Devastatingly merciless creatures that now prowled in endless numbers. Through every battle we have suffered, it seemed only our blood soaked the grounds beneath us. Many Warriors and casters of legendary tales have fought, and most have fallen. Not only our strength, but our hope has seemed to begin fading as well.

My weary eyes, covered in bloodied mud, weakening at the sights of wildfires infected with this evil essence. Flames of horror spread around the battlefield like a disease that cannot be cured. Lifeless bodies of fallen casters began to break down into dust, prior to fading away into the night skies. Weapons and armor, which belonged to those who have given and lost their very souls in this battle, decorated the trampled fields as their wielders spirit drifted from the living realm.

Even the stars were deeply reddened as if they were also stained with the blood of the fallen. Since the war has been waged, the night skies have never been the same. Storms formed, and the clouds were darker than ever. Countless souls have drifted beyond to the skies above. Their lives to be claimed by this unforgiving enemy, and souls to be put to rest in the heavens they followed.

Many fellow casters, brothers, and sisters to this homeland. Warriors of both blade and bow. Legends of battle, War Chiefs, and even common folk. They have all now become the heroes that stood when prayers of the innocent needed to be answered. They all have paid the ultimate sacrifice on this trail of blood and tears. Now, their energies have become ashes, and their stories of valor will be told.

Our selfless and righteous actions that have unceasingly been taken, now seems so miniscule. We rallied the flags of Nydeli. We have united nations that were at war for centuries. We marched the largest combined forces that Nydeli has ever borne witness, only to discover that our efforts may have still not been enough.

Approaching from the distance I could hear his villainous laughter. The rattling of broken chains that decorated his blood-stained armor. The screeching of his undead, flesh hungry ravens. This ancient enemy which was once just a fable, is now the source of death and destruction within our reality.

I was still attempting to find my ground after this enemy's last strike upon me. Even with all the bulging strength I yielded. Even with the immense power I have trained so hard to obtain. This enemy I faced still pummeled me around, as effortlessly as a leaf dances in the winds. There was still hope within my heart to fight, even at the cost of my own life.

My ancient gold trimmed, and deeply darkened obsidian armor had been shattered. Only the pauldrons remained, nearly cracked to dust but still draped upon my shoulders. The breastplate of my armor completely blown away from this enemies near fatal strike against me. Pieces of the obsidian had splintered into parts of my chest and abdomen.

I was pushing myself from the ground, blood gushing from my injuries. My ruby red, boiling blood was now drizzling the essence of war, as if my body were a canvas. Then, it was as if the battlefield itself drew silent. I could only hear this enemy's heinous laughter, echoing from everywhere within the fog around me. Shadows silhouetted so hastily that my eyes nearly missed his next move.

I drew my blades as fast as I could. Their holsters whistling the blood hungry ballad. The air itself splitting the fabric of nature as I crossed them in front of myself in a defensive stance. Only on one knee to ground myself against this battle-hardened dance.

Spearheading towards me, this unforgettable demon continued to challenge me. Within the blink of an eye, he swung his mighty Warhammer with vast power. On impact the clash was thunderous enough to quake Nydeli herself. If I were but an instant too late, such an assault could have drawn my last breath.

Such powers colliding created an explosion of magical energies between us. Yet again, I was sent crashing through the battlefields digging trenches with my own body. As I was plummeting through the war-stained and trampled meadows, I managed to find balance and dug my blades deeply into the ground to halt myself. With every bit of strength that remained, I dug my blades deeper into the soil of these lands.

The moment I was able to control myself and stop, my eyes were rattled from the sights of my blades. A webbed aura began illuminating from the very cores of both ancient and self-re-constructing steel fangs. This vile aura began to slowly consume the centuric structure of these violent weapons from wars of distant past.

In attempts to parry this enemy's last strike upon me, my ancient twin Dragokin Swords began to catastrophically shatter and fade to dust in the wind. Gales of battle whispered through the war zone, carrying the essence of thousands of battles, the gust swirling around, drifting away.

The intense explosion of energy from our collision created vibrations that rattled through my entire being. Travelling hastily, quivering uncontrollably from the impact endured through my own two blades. As I was trying to maintain strengthened grasp around their ceremoniously wrapped handles, I could feel ferocious shards digging harshly into my palms. Pain emerged from my bare hands. Blood now dripping from the historically decorated pommels. My hands became riddled with deepened cuts from the ancient steel these relics were forged with.

As my blades continued to crumble within my palms, I dropped what remained of the once valorous blades. I continued to bear witness as the ancient weapons I was bestowed were being reduced to mere splinters. Through the wars they have endured, through the legends they have created, it was but only this enemy's power that shattered the very steel Dragons themselves waged wars over.

I have become severely battered and maimed throughout the engagement with this enemy. His last assault against me, I could hardly defend against. My very being has been drained of what life and energies have fueled me, that have kept me fighting, breathing, and living. I felt completely defenseless now and unquestionably unarmed as I was finding my own breath. Then, as I was pushing myself from the bloodied mud beneath me, the fog around me split from this enemy's undying rush against me.

I had not been able to find my posture. War trampled mud still caked within and around my physically exhausted eyes. Blood continuously leaking from my gruesome injuries. There was near nothing that remained in my arsenal of defenses, even my own naturally inherited magical techniques were proving unaggressive results. With such haste that was conjured, I swung one arm systematically graphing their distinct patterns to hastily harvest a miniscule cluster of energies.

It was a last resort attempt to magically construct a life dependent barrier. Using but one hand I artistically created the symbol to manifest and cast a protective spell,

"**SCALE OF HENGTUIN!**" I casted just an instant before this enemy's warhammer could once again crush the entirety of my physical and even soulful being.

With one hand I was able to perfectly burst the grooved illumination of this long forgotten and forbidden spell, fierce dragon scales manifested from the fabrics of nature and magically widened methodically as dragon wings themselves. I forced what magical energies remained within the compartments of my very being to complete the spell so rapidly. As this enemy's warhammer crashed into the scaled barrier that magically came to be, yet another explosion of intangible energies burst forcibly in a violent tornado-like aura around us.

The pure unfathomable power from his attack brutally forced me to entrench the rock hardened grounds yet again. Only this time to gruesomely greet but one of the many massive boulders naturally scattered through the surface of these war-torn lands.

Historically peaceful countries which their own scholastic tomes of history will now carefully etch the devouring depictions of the devastating doom erupting through these inevitable battles. The meteoric craters and deepened trenches of war to forever imbalance the very structure of near undisturbed soils.

My back cracked vigorously and crumbled as I slammed against this harshly ridged boulder. Injuries of battle continuing to severely worsen as I was crushing deeper into the once sharpened shell of this cratering stone. While finely grinding to mere dust the very hardened structures of nature, my interest became piqued towards the remaining of my diminishing senses.

Rage boiled blood, slithering trails over the canvas of my rough scales and tanned skin. Gradually dripping down and around the sculpturing of my wide and hardened muscles. Lashing winds cooling the soaked and tattered clothes that barely endured under the concerning remains of armor. Ears screeching a high pitch ring as his villainous laughter hauntingly plagued the very air waves. My vision was slowly fading, flickering as a fire's light dances in the ghostly shadows. My body and mind were entirely throbbing with vicious and severe pain. The taste of blood, ashes, and earth infusing within the thickening streams abruptly spurting from my mouth.

I slid from the freshly carved crater, which was demolished through the suffering of my own body. My knees gruesomely collapsing as my face defeatedly splashed into bloodied puddles, of mud pooling below. Echoing sounds of war finding their melody within my ears as the ringing subtly settled. Thunderous war still waging, dying battle cries of familiars all circling around me. The unforgivable scent of this evil army only becoming more putrid.

Still, I denied the rumoring thoughts that this was truly to be the fate of our once heritage split world. I denied that fate itself was the only force able to trace the outlines of history. I denied the tales of old, all those in which projected prophecy of this worlds impending doom. Even so desperately grasping onto the edge of life itself, I denied the substantial difference of power between us and the enemies we faced.

Even the merciless weapons, those that our enemies fearlessly clenched onto, possessed unnatural strengths. This demons warhammer was unlike anything I have witnessed through my aged experiences of war. Toxic and vilely charcoaled streams of auras, dreadful magical energies emitted from the demons horrifying weapon. Souls of the fallen screamed from the warhammers darkly stained crystal pommel.

Viciously serrated teeth, seemingly extracted from mythical beasts that have been long extinct, protruded throughout the blood stained and twisted handle. Extending from grip to the anciently forged and violently shaped head. There was an awful organic aura that emitted from this weapon as well. I could only sense the deepest and darkest of evils from within it.

Deep down, I was now believing there would be but only one carefully conjured and highly forbidden technique. Such a magical possession to defeat this demon and the endless waves of battle hungering minions. That anything created by man, even ancient weaponry from the distant past, was not going to scathe this demon or change the momentum of battle.

That even an almighty and divine strike would only be a possible infliction to bring this enemy to its knees. There was but one spell that I believed- could send this enemy to his grave. This power that could be called upon, would certainly fold the pages of my story as well.

If calling upon this mystical power should end this demon, my own life over Nydeli's fate should not be placed upon the same scale. I could only hope that with such action taken, the future of this world may be secured for many generations to come. This enemy, an enemy unlike any other that I have faced in the past. An enemy only heard of within frightful tales. I feared the risk I would need to take. For the fate of the world solely lied upon my next move.

"Your world crumbles beneath your feet and your allies have fallen. Before I send this world into a dark abyss, you shall understand the true power I behold. Feel honored young Dragon, for your eyes are about to be the only ones to witness ancient magic at its peak." the dark voice boasted through the thick fog of war.

My injuries were horrifically severe. I spit a puddle of blood from my mouth and mustered the strength to reply, "Demon, you underestimate my strength, and your ego sickens me. To think you have already won the war when this battle is not yet over. We may have suffered in numbers along your trail of chaos, but the ones whom remain standing have hearts that still beat with everlasting life, and the inferno of war that burns inside myself is greater than that of all the stars above."

It took every ounce of strength within me to get back onto my feet. Blood endlessly spouting from the gruesome injuries that had been inflicted upon me. The battle against this demon had taken a fatal toll against those who stood and fought. Those with pure hearts that did not retreat in the face of malicious evil. I was looking around, reaching my very heart through the battlefields, only to notice there were none of those familiar souls for my own to find.

The minions that followed this demon surrounded our battle in vast numbers. Their silhouettes flailed around within the heavy fog that consumed the smoke suffocated battlefield. Horrific creatures that ascended from the darkest of pits in the demon's quake. Creatures that have been dormant since the Dawn of the New Age. Immortally rumored beasts that were sealed away only by the combined forces of ancient and forbidden magic.

As I was regaining myself, I began to subtly recognize those familiar souls' I was searching for. My senses could feel their essence in the vast distance. I could feel many of their energies fading. Battle cries echoing through the fields as if we were within a silent tunnel. I did not want to believe my allies were falling to this demon. I did not want to believe that every effort made thus far, had been for nothing.

At that moment, it was my heart which suffered the most. The thought of my allies, my friends, and my family being claimed by this Demons vile crusade. Knowing that our stories will be lost within the sands of time. That this demon was going to destroy everything we have fought for over the years. This could not be the end of our world, the world as we knew it.

His shadow now appeared through the fogs. "No young Dragon, what sickens me is the poor excuse of a fight that the **Sinaunang Dragon Ng Propesiya** (*Ancient Dragon of Prophecy*) had prepared for me. Of all the prophecies, this day, this battle, was just a tall tale, a meaningless fable. No matter, this world's end is now!" the dark voice proclaimed as magical energies began to wisp around his hand reaching for the skies.

A blackened aura began to consume the clouds above. Lightning filled the skies, and thunder roared across the battle forged lands. What little light that-was exposed, was now painted black. Dark matter began to rain from the skies. The minions that followed this demon were now being sent into a rage. Howling and screeching towards the skies, much like rabid animals during a Blood Moon.

I could sense not only the demon's energies rising, but the minions that followed this foe were also becoming stronger. It was as if this demon cracked the barrier between our world and theirs. That this change in the atmosphere, the blackened aura, and the dark matter, were the source of their power. I could not accept that their world would surely consume ours.

Before my own eyes, absolute horror had been revealed. I witnessed the souls of the fallen become engulfed by the blackened aura. The magical energies leading these souls to the Halls of the Heavens were quickly ignited with vile green flames. This dark matter that poured from the skies, this evil brought upon us, was defiling even the faith of divinity. My heart ached at the thought that those brave souls will forever be lost.

As this demon before me lifted his murderous warhammer, the fallen began to pull towards it. Once immaculate, brightened orbs of pure souls, were now poisoned with this vile green aura. Their luminescent figures crying out to be saved as they were slowly becoming consumed by this enemy's weapon. As each soul was devoured, the aura from the weapon pulsed intensely with unbelievable strength. Such a vile essence personally witnessed, would undeniably poison the hearts of those around.

This demon began laughing once again. The voices of those who were becoming consumed now echoing his laughter. As this demon's power and energies were escalating, his silhouette within the fog continued to grow as well. He spread his six wings widely, and whirlpools of gust slashed through the fogs. Sounds of snapping as his natural melody dashed towards me while harmonizing his villainous laugh.

To think this enemy possessed such power. A power that even denied that of the heavens. I could not stand by any longer and witness those brave souls be denied everything they have fought and fallen for. The only way to end it all, was to become the very force that started it all……...

My eyes suddenly burst open. Widening as such haunting images vanished, and day's new light broke in. It was but only a deep slumber I was subdued within. My body was shivering to the bones, and face drenched in hot, never-ending beads of sweat. My heart, beating faster than the echo of war drums. I was only dreaming, yet it all felt surreal. The pain I bore, the vile scent of a war-torn battlefield, the ear shattering cries of all my fallen comrades.

I was only convinced of being back within the living realm upon witnessing the day's fresh sunlight creeping through the windows of my room. As I was regaining my own senses, sweet aromas were now relieving my airways. There was now solitude within the silence of this room. There was no longer pain, only the comfort found within my home.

This dream had shaken me from my slumber. Its message unclear, but the images painted within my mind would forever be vivid. I have yet to experience something this surreal. These thoughts may ponder, but for the time being, I must deal with the here and now. I must regain peace within my heart and mind.

My mind broke from such rattling thoughts as I felt her tiny plush toes tenderly brushing against my scaled legs. Then, she slowly turned within her slumber and wrapped her delicate and soft thigh around my own rough and heavily scarred skin. Her gentle hand slid slowly from my scarred abdomen to my battle marked chest. Even within her slumber, she gripped me ever so lovingly. Such actions restored the purest and utmost warmest of thoughts within my mind.

With eyes still heavy, beside me I witnessed the love of my life safely curled up. Sleeping ever so soundlessly. I softly brushed her silky hazel hair behind her delicate little ear. The emerald charms in which decorated her ears shimmered as beams of sunlight reflected from them. My heart was fluttering as her unmatched beauty was unveiled. The peace in which my love displayed was surely the beautiful image my mind desperately sought.

Before I wrapped my arm around her to secure her warmth against my hardened chest, my claws gently traced the ceremonial arts stained within her arms. I began to subtly stretch. My wings slowly extending, the muscles within my own heavily black and reddened stained chest and shoulders tightening. As my legs extended underneath the sheets, my feet met an unmovable lump near the edge of our bed. I peeked towards the edge to find yet another reason to fill my heart with peace and joy.

My trusted companion was also found to be fast asleep. Her wings tucked tightly against her body. It seemed as if she may also be experiencing a dream. Her ears twitching, paws paddling away, and she was subtly nibbling within her slumber. This brought humor to me. That she may be dreaming of a glorious hunt. That the dream realm is challenging her physical abilities.

I rolled to the edge of the bed, sluggishly, to avoid waking both my love and faithful companion. As I sat there, I could not help but to witness the serenity my dearest displayed in her sweet and soundless slumber. Such beauty has always been unknown to me until I met her. Still, I wondered how such an innocent and caring soul could find love within the beast that I was.

I removed myself from the bed and proceeded towards the window. Bare as the day I was brought into this world, I wrapped around my hips a silky sheet that draped from the edge of our bed. Slowly, I pulled the curtains aside that swept within the window to expose the most beautiful overlook upon the City of Flame Thorn. My house atop the only mountain in miles. Not only am I one of the protectors of this luminating city but also the guardian to the heart beating deeply within these mountains.

Sweat continued to slowly bead down my chiseled and chipped face. These warm beads dripping along the scars that gashed my chin. Dripping aggressively down my bare, scaled, and highly ceremoniously branded and marked chest.

Looking out to the scenery of the silver glistening mountains helped to remind me there is still peace within this world. That the creatures of Nydeli harmonize while the days new light brings warmth. There was no reason to be so immensely shook from the dream I had just experienced.

Chakra, my trusted companion for as long as I can remember, awakened shortly after me. Her wings spread with an illustrious stretch. Eyes squinting as she crawled out of the bed. She soon accompanied me by the window. While nuzzling her head against my ribs, she too joined my endless gaze over the city. Chakra always knew when I was troubled. The bond we shared was greater than any throughout Nydeli.

"It felt so real Chakra. My dream was so vivid, and I felt devastation within my heart." I whispered as I used my claws to scratch behind her tall ears.

Chakra was a Mythical beast, the last of a dying breed. Dragon hound, a creation between the great wolves and mystical dragons. These mythical beasts have wandered this world for almost as long as dragons themselves. They have brilliant minds from birth, and already understand the world for what it is. I was lucky to have her by my side for the amount of time we have shared thus far.

We have faced many challenges together, and still to this day, I believe the only reason Chakra and I formed such a strong bond was because we both have dragon's blood running through our veins. That we were destined to share our path with one another. She leaned her head upon me and gave out a subtle yet deepened howl.

I vowed to Chakra as I continued to scratch her neck, "Calm down girl there is nothing to worry about. You two ladies I will protect with my life itself," then Chakra looked over at my love with the look of jealousy in her eyes. "You do not have to envy her. She is one with us, just as we were for so long. Let us gather some fresh food to place upon the table. That is surely to put you in a better mood."

As I stopped scratching Chakra's neck, her leg halted from twitching. I turned from the window to gather my armor. The distinguished gold trimmed and obsidian armor shining brilliantly as the day's new light reflected from it. This armor was one of a kind, truly worthy of my kin's reputation. The historical symbol of my kin etched into the chest plate of such honorably forged and flawlessly riveted sheets of metal. I was but the only living being to bear such an emblem, it lived to symbolize the bloodline that shall never be forgotten.

My love's soft, gentle voice serenaded my ears as I was wrapping an ancient War Chiefs sash around my arm. "Where are you two heading out for so early?" she asked as she completely revealed her unrivaled beauty from under the sheets.

Her long, luscious hair cascaded down her bare chest. Her angel like skin glowing like a sunset's reflection on gentle tides. Her eyes shimmering the most beautiful opalescent shades as the streams of sunlight met them. Her cheeks soon to be blushed once her astonishing eyes met mine.

For a moment, I was breathless. I believe she was an angel sent from above. To guide me away from darkness. To lead my heart in the direction opposite of absolute destruction. To breathe the purest of life into my soul. The love I yielded for her was that of the strongest... Unbreakable.

"We are going out to hunt and gather food for the day ahead of us. We will be back shortly." I proclaimed while placing one hand upon her soft, blushed cheek, and pressing my lips firmly against hers.

Her lips were the softest that mine have ever met. They tasted sweeter than the finest of honey throughout all the lands. She slowly wrapped her hands around my neck, pulling me deeper within her presence. We embraced one another in this deepened kiss momentarily, finding serenity within one another. Her heart fluttered as our lips were lusciously locked together. I could sense her intentions were to keep me there in that moment.

Though I was content, though I wanted to get lost within her soul, though I yearned for the continuation of her seductively gentle touch, I knew I needed to break from her ever so affectionate spell. As I hesitantly pulled away from her indisputably intoxicating aura, her fingertips gradually pressured against my neck, gliding heavily down my back. I released from the kiss we were almost bound within, and I knew she would yield words to follow.

"Must you leave now?" She whispered as her gentle hands made unceasing attempts to pull me back into her seductive grip.

"The sands of time only dribble my love, there is not a crisis that forces our concerns now. I must clear my thoughts before this day moves forward." I replied as my own firm grip indecisively loosened from around her curvaceous hips.

"If you are to leave, take heed to my words. I know you prefer both of your swords, but you worry me without your shield. Take it, please." She pleaded as she placed her hands upon mine.

    She grabbed one of my hands and gently nestled her cheek within my palm. Then, she closed her eyes and buried herself within my chest. I chuckled but for a moment and cradled her within my arms. Brushing her ever so softened hair as she continued to find comfort within my presence. Upon reopening her eyes, her gaze met my own and we almost became lost.
    She hesitantly pushed from my cherishing grip around her. It seemed there was the slightest of pouting within her eyes and upon her lips. The realization begun to timidly settle that even with her admirable efforts, she could not keep me within her seductive trance. She crawled to my side of the bed, allowing what little sheets still covered her body, to expose her beauty entirely.

I was fighting the urge to completely ravish her and find myself back within her lustful warmth, she turned for a moment and chuckled at the sight of my own internal fight. After she was pleased with teasing my temptations, she wrapped herself completely back within our silky sheets. Then, she reached underneath our bed.

She needed both hands to slide the mighty tower shield, covered in dust, from underneath our bed. Such an impenetrable object she had acquired for me so long ago. This shield was an ancient relic. From the wars of the past. Only the fiercest of Warriors had claimed its true power. As she struggled with the weight of the mighty shield, I chuckled for a moment before grabbing it from her and slinging it across my back.

I admiringly confessed as she softly cradled her chin within my palm again, "Your eyes are my weakness, my love, and you know this."

Chakra glared at us with her own piercing eyes, as if my love ignored the fact that Chakra has protected me almost my entire life. Chakra knew I did not need to wield a shield because her wings provided me with greater fortification. As my dearest wrapped her soft and silky arms around me, Chakra left the room with her head held high. We could tell she scoffed at the interactions between my love and myself.

"You have made her mad again," I humored.

"I hope she knows I am not trying to replace her. Earning Chakra's love is harder than earning the trust of the elders." Her sweet and gentle words concerned with a subtle whimpering tone.

"She has been with me since our younger days, and you know this. We have grown together and fought together. My swords are for her, as she is for me. We bleed together and cry together. We walk the same path until our dying breath. Someday she will learn to love you as she loves me." I reminded my love while equipping the remainder of my armor.

Again, with a concerned tone she replied, "I hope so."

Gently, she released her nurturing grip from around me. She then returned underneath the pelt of a fallen chimera that I had slain in the past. I could not help but to watch her for a moment, because through her I found peace and love. If not for her, I may not be the Dragokin I am today. As I left the room, I sneakily grabbed my second sword while she was snuggling herself in the sheets.

"Let us go Chakra. There is some food that needs to be placed upon our table." She replied with a mighty howl.

Life was not always this calm and enjoyable. I once did not know what love was, or even the path of a civilized life. There were points in my life where I was alone or lost. I did not have any allies, nor as many foes as I have today. I want to take you on the journey that has been my life thus far and allow you the opportunity to walk in my footsteps. I will not leave out any details and I will give you all that I behold knowledge to. My name is Drago Bonez, a Dragokin from the clan Roaming Lance Force, and this is my story:

CHAPTER TWO
The Path Forged in Flames

It was at the sight of the day's new light in which unsealed my eyes. At either side of me laid Mother and Father, both of their hands meeting one another gently, while rested upon my rounded stomach. I stretched, and my wings must have brushed the both of them, because I could feel them begin to stir out of their slumber.

Mother chuckled as she revealed her luminous silver eyes, "It seems someone is beginning to learn from their **Father**."

Father rustled awake, he slowly gripped me with his claws and pulled me up on the crimson reddened scales decorating his chest, "If **I** am not mistaken, only hunters prove themselves during such early hours of the days."

"**Only** hunters that are **old** enough to prove themselves at such early hours of the day, **my dear**." Mother snickered as she was attempting to break me from Father's grip.

Father's garnet wings began to slowly wrap around us. "Ah yes my love, I remember when I was but his age as well. You two should join me on the hunt this morning. Allow him to begin witnessing the world for what it is. If you shelter him too long, surely he will fall behind that of others his age." Father replied as his wings constricted and dawned around us.

We were all still so tired, shaking the heaviness of slumber from our beings. Mother began to playfully prevent Father's wings from wrapping around us. He just chuckled at her own display of early morning tiresome strength. Fathers early waking strength proved a bit more overwhelming. As Mother battled Father, his wings locked around only him and I. The suns rising light diminished as his red leathery wings condensed, now it was only the deeply reddened aura within his eyes that I could witness.

As Father's wings dawned over us, we could hear the muffled tones of Mother snickering, "What are you doing? Do **not** tempt our child's young and innocent mind!"

"You hear that my Dragon? That is your Mother bickering about out there. If she only knew how much I yearned to begin your training," Father whispered as Mother was attempting to breach the shell of his wings, "We both care for you deeply, but our expectations are quite different from one another. I want to bring you for a hunt; therefore, she shelters you. She wishes you to be a scholar, whereas I wish for you to be…."

Before Father could finish confessing, Sharpened silver claws broke through the once thought impenetrable shell of his tough red wings. Days light now beaming into the shadow that we were. We both laid there as we could witness a subtle rage within her burning silver eyes. She stood above us vigilantly, and a subtle metallic aura was flickering around her being. She was huffing and puffing while breaching his once locked wings, yet he did not bead sweat as she seemed to be.

"**Uh oh**. It seems your Mother is…" Father chuckled before Mother sliced his words quiet.

"*It seems your Mother is….* **What**?" Mother hastily mimicked.

"Quisvale, I was but only…." He attempted with words that would have been sent towards with question.

"*Quisvale, I was but only….* **Nothing**, now give me my child!" Mother impersonated and sneered towards him again.

"*A Warrior.*" Father whispered to me while hesitantly extending me towards Mother.

"Now that you have challenged me, I think it is best you gather some more food and supplies for the coming days, my love." Mother snapped towards him while she gently secured me to her hip, tenderly pulling only her and I from the comfort of our bed.

"Yes, my dearest, first I must handle precious matters within the village. The elders spoke from concern yesterday. There is a **gathering**." Father replied. Once, there was humor within his heart, but slowly there began to emerge his own grave concern.

He too was pulling himself from his side of the bed. Father's wings stretched wide as his shadow casted heavily within our home. Tiresomely stumbling within chunks of leather and darkened steel clumped around the claws that were his feet. Mother was soon to stop dead in her tracks, as I gripped firmly against her sensing the tension in the room.

"*A gathering?*" Mother glanced with her own questionable whisper.

She broke from her slight anger that in which steered us from his side. Then, she found her delicate hands helping Father. Gradually securing the weathered leather wraps around his arms and back. Constricting the heavy armor around his scarred skin. The seemingly heavy, blackened plates of obsidian armor that draped over his broadened shoulders always looked immaculate.

As those two cooperated in fluent harmony, I sensed a deepened love while they continued to finely adjust his armor. My own hands now rebelling from their shared task and brushing against the rough hardened surface of immensely charcoaled obsidian. Smooth rippled bumps and riddled grooves proving only colder as my fingertips traced deepened gashes of battle.

"Yes, they did not speak much upon it. Only that we are to discuss such matters with Draxxux and the elders." Father graved sternly as he strapped anciently designed sheathes to a heavy leathered belt.

"Though you have raised my own concern, this does not break the battle you have waged this morning. **Remember that**." Mother declared whilst sharing his tone.

After Father fully dawned within the gold trimmed relentless armor, sliced aura emitting double-edge blades into their sheathes, and shook his balance true, he grabbed Mothers hands and heavily surrendered, "You have won this battle, yet this **war** is not over."

    Mother and Father both found the slightest of humor from within his words. She did not appear to be as impressed while his own darkened ruby eyes displayed comfort. His natural intimidating glare broke from our eyes, and he trailed stoically towards the door. I sensed their hearts yielded more wholesome intentions, especially between one another, but nothing was spoken aloud or physically hinted.

    Father finished with securing a darkened sash bearing ancient designs around his arm. A savagely decorated obsidian symbol swung heavily around his neck, clanking against his armor. Then, without returning sights upon us, he proceeded his path departing from our home.

It was only after Father's departure that Mother snappishly found herself scattered within our home. She was soon to carefully position me onto the honey polished wooden floors. Young minded and yet far from fully aged, so I was still unable to confidently find my true balance. I would always exhaustingly crawl around on both my hands and feet.

Desperately trailing nearest her path. Often to be found as in obstacle within her claws intended steps. She would flawlessly stretch her gray scaled legs around me. Even before I could brokenly enclose my bare bone wings defensively around myself.

Mother was preparing elegantly steaming and well-proportioned dishes. The most delicate and tangy scents were whipping around our home as she mixed many foods together. The food she prepared was always so delicious. Was always so intoxicatingly decorated on the plates. Just the steamy sight and sizzling scent of such exquisite pleasantries sent my mouth into a salivating rage. As if every portion she has ever prepared were to nourish every hungering stomach within distance.

As I usually attempted to stand on my own two feet, my arms could be found steadying myself on everything within reach. This time it happened to be Mothers smooth legs. She quickly took notice to my knee trembling balance. She stopped arranging the food on the plates and shook her hands dry.

Within moments like these she would burst with heart-felt joy and gut weakening humor. My legs began wobbling out of control the higher my claws reached and pulled myself from the ground. The weight of my wings alone was the heaviest of personal and physical burdens during this time of my life.

As I continued exhausting the remaining essence of strength that I had, flapping my wings through the intense pressure shocking through my body, I soon fell back and Mother gasped, "Be careful my child, for you must first find your balance before finding your ground."

After Mother brushed me off, she picked me up and placed me on a coarse yet comfortably cushioned pelt. She then grabbed the dishes she was preparing, with such incomparable of scents still whipping around our home. Mother sat next to me and the moment she placed the dish within my claws grasp, I begun devouring the hot and smoking food at a vicious pace. I was making such a mess of myself, and Mother had not even touched her own food yet. Mother just laughed, witnessed, and observed as I was figuring out how to consume every last bit.

"There is still much in this world you must learn my Dragon, and forever will you be a hatchling within my eyes. Your Father's love is thick, and he just wants to see you grow into the Dragon we wish for you to become." Mother said as she started wiping my face from the mess I had turned myself into, "Though your Father and I have faced many battles together, I do not wish for that to become your life, if that is not what you so choose."

As Mother was speaking to me, I could not help but to get lost within her brightly luminescent eyes. They sparkled as beams of sunlight danced within them. As if they were the purest of silver rivers smelted from Hengtuin's flames. The varying shades of streams swirled so elegantly together. Such eyes felt as if they not only sought your heart and soul, but also mended those in the sights of such beauty.

With a mouth full of food, and stomach bulging even more so, I pushed the plate from in front of me and threw myself back onto the pelt. I just laid there on the ground admiring Mother for everything she was. As she sat there and returned her own loving glance, her heart began to flutter. Such warmth emitting from her very soul, it could even be felt by all those around.

Mother chuckled momentarily and then began feasting upon her own food with carefully thought intentions. As I continued to watch Mother, I was growing overwhelmingly tiresome from the belly filling feast I sloppily finished before her. My eyes began to battle their own will to remain open. My head swaying from side to side. Mother took joyous notice to everything I would do.

Once she was finished with enjoying her plate, she slid both hers and mine to the side. Using the very worn cloths wrapped around her, she wiped her hands and face clean. Then, her nurturing hands found my chubby sides and she picked me up. She nestled us together as we found ourselves retracing steps towards the warmth found within our bed.

Before my eyes finally won the battle, Mother whispered ever so softly as she slid a weighted blanket over me, "Do not fight it my Dragon, allow your body and mind to rest."

The dream I experienced within my slumber was nothing out of the ordinary. Memories jumbled together emerging within my mind skit by skit. Memories of my life leading up to the present. From times that Mother would grab both of my hands and pull me onto my own feet:

"Soon enough my Dragon, you will be creating your own footprints that will mark history itself,"
Mother would chant cheerfully,
"Almost there, give me but two more steps."

Memories of Mother and Father preparing our meals together. Playfully nudging one another as it seemed they were in competition,

"To think I bewedded a man who has forgotten how to prepare a delicate meal,"
Mother would snicker as Father seemed to be struggling over any dish he attempted to make,

"Come now, War Chief, surely you remember how you impressed me so long ago."

To the simple and joyful nights that we would share with one another. Comforted next to an open fire, within one another's presence, just enjoying the essence between us all,

"Quisvale, we sure have changed from our younger days,"
Father would preach as his gaze would bounce from Mother to myself,
"and to think, now we are raising our own child together. How far we have come from delinquents in the thoroughfares."

Soon, my eyes began to twitch, and I woke from the quick slumber I was subdued within. With heavy eyes, I witnessed Mother lying next to me. She had one hand rested upon my belly again, as I usually found it to be so. It seemed Father had not returned home yet. I did not want to leave the bed quite yet either, so I rolled over and clenched onto Mother's arm.

As I was lying there, I took notice to the scars that marked Mothers arms. What were once deepened gashes of battle, now hardened blemishes that proved her strength. My hands slowly traced these scars. My own claws finely etching where blades once cut so deeply. Mother realized I was awake again and broke from her slumber.

"Once a Shield Maiden, now just a Mother to my precious Dragon," Mother whispered as she began pinching my cheeks, "it seems we both should waken before your Father returns and realizes that we have achieved nothing."

Mother wrapped me within her arms and embraced me in a warm and loving hold. While Mother was kissing my cheeks, I began to erupt in laughter. Attempting to push away from her nurturing caress. Once Mother was finished, she placed me back onto the bed and wrapped me up with the soft pelt that spread across.

"I shall gather some fresh fruits to fuel you, my Dragon. I will not be gone long." Mother said before she kissed me once more and prepared herself for departure.

I just laid there on the bed, watching as Mother began to grab a carefully woven basket and spear. She elegantly wrapped a silken robe around her and began towards the door. Before Mother left, she glanced back at me once more. Mother waved a kiss towards me and then proceed from our home.

I laid there on the bed for longer than I expected to. Long enough to cause my body and mind to feel exhausted once more. I rolled around a while and slapped my hands against the bed, the most entertainment I could find within my loneliness. I only could do such for so long though before I was yet again fighting the urge to sleep.

Slowly, and heavily, my eyes began to seal shut again. I fought for as long as I could. Lifting my head from the slow collapse. Swaying my sights from side to side. Wiping my eyes in attempts to keep them open. It was a lost battle, and I was soon to fall unconscious.

The dream realm had been visiting more often as I grew older, as I was now beginning to try and understand life. My mind was expanding from the emptiness in which it was, to understand the essence that makes us beings. To understand love and the very meaning of our souls. To understand, everything:

"I do not know why you shelter him as immensely as you do Quisvale, others his age are already flourishing in the school yards and our child has yet to speak."
Father would argue as he would fully tilt a mug of ale.

*"He is not just any child, Charmortus, he is **our** child. Do not ignore such a fact."*
Mother snapped back.

"Yes, but there is nothing to fear my love. The past is the past, we made the decisions. We cannot fear what could become, we must embrace what this path…..."
Father sluggishly slurred into his own sudden slumber.

Intense streams of light broke my mind from the dream realm. As I slowly broke my eyes from their crusted seals, I realized the suns brilliant light was becoming overwhelmed by the moons own ghostly glow.

I was still alone on the bed. There was no Mother, no Father. I could hear the wooden panels on our house creaking. There was a subtle breeze brushing through, lashing the sheets in the windows. As I was wiping my weighted eyes, I continued scanning the darkness that our home was now becoming. It seemed there was no one to be sought.

Then, a loud crash from outside was quick to pull my wakening attention. I focused my eyes shakenly in that direction. Then, again, another loud crash approaching closer to our home. There were unfamiliar voices muffled by the hollowed breeze. I could hear thickened chains rattling around now, and the familiar sounds of sharpened weapons clanking against one's armor. I broke from the sheet Mother wrapped me in and crawled backward, away from the approaching sounds.

The sound of footsteps mixed with the loud clashing sounds of things being smashed outside. A choked and villainous laughter erupted from whomever was causing such a havoc. It seemed they had become more intrigued with our home, because I could hear the clatter and their raucous voices growing louder. Something here must have piqued their interest.

I could now see the flickering of a torch pacing around the perimeter of our home. The flames were dancing, beams of light were now bouncing between the cracks in our walls, seeping into the darkness I was consumed in. Slowly this light moved directly in front of the door. Then, suddenly, it burst open, breaking from the hinges.

Within the doorway stood two Dwarven men. Fresh blood painted amongst their faces, dripping down their beards and oozing off their weapons. One wielded a mighty axe. Whilst the axe was stretched across his shoulders, in his other hand was the torch. The second Dwarven man wielded a mighty crossbow, with three bolts readily available. It seemed they dripped of a toxic ooze, as the bolts dribbled this ooze unto the ground, smoke emitted from the points of impact.

These Dwarves were decorated as if they were ready for war. Heavy armor shielded their pudgy bodies, marks of blades and battle etched within the very metals. There was a potent and pungent smell emitting from their beings. The hostility coated within the air itself was thick. Surely their intentions and being here were not that of friendly nature. As they were scanning our home, their eyes were soon to meet my own shaken gaze.

"Well, who is to stop us no……" the Dwarf with the mighty axe muttered before a spear protruded through his chest.

Blood spouted from the Dwarves' injury, and he immediately fell to the ground. The torch that was clenched in his hand quickly ignited our doorway in flames. As the fire blazed and climbed up the entryway, the other Dwarf was sent into a panic. He was stumbling around his dying comrade, slipping on the fresh puddle of blood. He readied his crossbow, hands trembling from what was becoming of their situation.

An almighty war cry burst from outside, such a deepened roar sent chills even down my own spine. The Dwarf, in panic, readied his crossbow and began launching bolts. One at a time these bolts would emit a vile green aura and then, with close to unrecognizable speeds, they barraged. A burst of pain stopped the fearsome battle cry, and soon I learned why.

"What the fu..." the second Dwarf said as he was tackled through the doorway.

It was Mother, she had charged the Dwarf head on and tackled him through the doorway. Mothers body was surrounded by a silver aura, and within her eyes I witnessed true, untamable rage. There were two bolts pierced through Mother's arm, her own blood gushing as they engaged in close quartered combat.

Mother was soon to break from her enemy and created distance between them. They both were attempting to posture and prepare for another engagement. The Dwarf seemed to have gripped two blades that were readily holstered to his hips. Mother gruesomely ripped the two serrated arrows from her suddenly gushing arm, positioning herself for an offensive approach.

Our home was quickly filling with smoke. Mother positioned her hands in front of her, gripping tightly onto the blood dripping bolts, prepared for the next strike. As they slowly paced around, Mother found her stance close to me. She took up a defensive posture while spreading her wings wide. It was hard for me to see beyond Mother and the smoke.

"You think you can stop us?! We have already breached your precious…." The Dwarf began shouting.

Just before the Dwarf could finish what he was saying, a deeply blackened shadow rose from behind him. This shadow slowly began to outline that of a Dragokin. Then, within the blink of an eye, the blackened shadow wrapped around the Dwarf and silenced him forever. The Dwarf fell from the concealment of the shadow and hit the ground as blood was oozing from his neck.

"M'Lady, Charmortus sent us to rally you and your child. We must leave!" the shadowed figure said with its deep and cracked voice.

Shortly after it spoke, the blackened shadow began to whirl around. The fire and smoke that was spreading and burning through our home was being pulled towards this being. Once the flames were doused and the smoke was cleared, the shadow began to transform. The once smokey vapor now solidifying into an elderly, crouched Dragokin.

"I am thankful for your arrival. If I was but a moment too late…" Mother confessed before the other ravenous elder Dragokin cut her off,

"No time for gratitude M'Lady Quisvale, grab your child." He said to Mother as he turned from our doorway and left our home underneath the shadows of what seemed to be one hundred crows.

Mother was quick to turn and find me still sitting upon our bed. Her eyes were filled with tears and her heart filled with pain. I grew concerned for Mother because I have never seen her in such a condition before. I then reached my arms towards her, and she lunged towards me with haste.

"Never again my Dragon, shall I leave you alone," Mother confessed as she wrapped her arms around me.

As Mother's tears were soaking my shoulders, she began to wrap me around her own body. Tucking me tightly and covering my head and wings. There was not much I could see after she had wrapped me the way she had. There was but only a sliver over Mother's shoulder that I could bear witness through. Mother began pacing around our home, and then another voice emerged,

"M'Lady, the Shadows are leading a way through the Mountains by order of the Chief. We must move now."

"Please, send word to Charmortus and relieve his mind that we are safe. I am but grabbing a few things and we shall be on the trail shortly," Mother pleaded. As it sounded, she was equipping her own valorous armor.

"Yes M'Lady. I will send but one to advise the Chief. The remainder of us were appointed as your detail," Another stoic voice responded.

After a short while I could see that we were now leaving our home. In the great distance I could see massive fires spread throughout the lands. Being outside I could now hear the sounds of war. The loudest sound was the thundering cries and panic of the retreating masses. It was too dark to bear witness to our numbers, but from the noise alone, I felt there were thousands rushing around us.

I began to wiggle from the concealing wrap Mother had tightened around me. As I was wiggling about, Mother would attempt to cover me again. Through the darkness I could only see the dancing of massive flames in the vast distance. The moonlight was beginning to reveal all those around.

Warriors, scholars, nobles, and common folk. Hundreds amongst thousands of Dragokin all retreating towards the mountains. I finally broke from the concealment Mother continued to wrap me within, only to bear witness to destruction. As all the others continued to retreat, Mother stood atop a hill that overlooked all below.

"M'Lady, the War Chief will be with us shortly. We must continue. The 2nd Command will now serve as our people's shield," a brute Dragokin wielding two mystical axes urged.

"Let her be brother, for we never know when we shall see our lands again. We should too take in this moment with our Shield Maiden," another brute Dragokin said to the first as he rested a mighty sword upon his shoulder.

"We have secured a path to the coastline as directed, for within the shadows we shall stay hidden," whispered a shadowy being now seeping through from Nydeli's surface.

"The prophecy is beginning to unfold, Warriors, until the Dragons of Legend return, our homes will be forever lost." Mother said as tears began to roll down her cheek.

As we sat atop this hill, the fires only continued to spread throughout our lands. The weeping of those around began to trail in the winds. Mother stood in the position as a few Warriors accompanied her endless gaze over the hell flamed valley. Each Warrior was decorated differently, with varying armor and weapons. Then, as another Dragokin equipped with a massive bow approached Mother, she began to sing, and this song began to echo from all those retreating through the battle forged and shadow infested mountains,

"Ang mundo ay huwad ng kanyang apoy at sinaktan ng kanyang mga pakpak,
(*The world was forged by his fire and struck by his wings,*)

Ang aming mga giyera at kwento sa buhay ang mga kantang nais niyang kantahin,
(*Our wars and life stories are the songs he wants to sing,*)

Ang lupain ng mga Dragon na pinatibay upang makatiis sa anumang paglabag,
(*The land of Dragons fortified to withstand any breach,*)

Kung saan ang lahat ng mga Dragon ay umunlad sa ilalim ng proteksyon ng kanyang maabot,
(*Where all Dragons thrive under the protection of his reach,*)

Nasa atin ang kanyang pagpapala kaya't nabubuhay at namamatay tayo sa pamamagitan ng kanyang apoy,
(*We have his blessing so we live and die by his fire,*)

Ang dugo ng mga Dragon sa loob ng ating mga ugat na nagbibigay ng ilaw sa ating sariling mga pyres,
(*It is the blood of Dragons within our veins that gives light to our own pyres,*)

Magpakailanman ang aking Dragon ay aakyat at masasaksihan mo ang iyong sariling kaluwalhatian,
(*Forever my Dragon will ascend and you will witness your own glory,*)

Magpakailanman ang aking Dragon ay maghahari at magiging isang scholar ng kanyang sariling kwento!"
(*Forever my Dragon will reign and be a scholar of his own story!*)

CHAPTER THREE
The Unveiled Truth

Even though the retreat was being guided by Warriors, it seemed all those around were still lost. The moon light provided us with what light it could, which revealed within their eyes a sense of lost hope. Father had yet to return to us and I could sense Mother knew deeply within her own heart, that these people, our people, needed guidance. They needed reassurance from a leader of prestige.

As we continued this retreat forced upon us, not only I, but also Mother, took great notice that this journey was becoming more soiled with the blood, sweat, and tears of those around. Thousands of Dragokin were forced to retreat from their homelands. Mother carried me tightly against her hip, but over her shoulders I could still witness and sense the pain within those around us.

The path through the mountains was rough, and surely it was taking a toll on this caravan. It seemed we were avoiding any path already trodden. The path we created was freshly carved into these mountains. Some Dragokin had the strength to soar above, but most were far to restless and tiresome to make such attempts at flying. This approach of staying off the beaten roads seemed to be the best option, regardless the harsh conditions.

As my eyes were wandering, I noticed there were many who displayed the misfortune of battle. There were Medicus Dragokin scattering throughout the crowds, finding those who desperately needed their attention. Pulling them to the side one by one to tend to their wounds. As this was happening, some were harnessing magical abilities to tend to the injured, others utilizing physical medical techniques. Compared to the vast numbers of the injured, the Medicus Dragokin were surely overwhelmed.

There was but one Medicus Dragokin that followed within the group of Warriors that paced carefully by Mother's side. He seemed to be the leader of the few that focused on the crowds. They came to him for orders, and they would soon scurry off back into the trail of our kin.

This Dragokin bore many scars of battle himself, much more than his Medicus counterparts. The Medicus Dragokin urging through the crowds were but only dawned in white garbs. Whereas this Medicus, he was heavily armored within brightened steel that seemed to be trimmed with emeralds and rubies.

These Dragokin that followed so closely were the same Warriors that stood with Mother and I along the hilltop before our true retreat into the Mountains. They all held themselves stoically, hands itching at their weapons. Each of these Warriors nearby Mother seemed to be of higher prestige than all the remaining around. Their eyes were steadily scanning our surroundings.

I began depicting each of these Warriors that followed closely to Mother. Each of these Dragokin seemed to display their own fearsome look. Few of these Dragokin were heavily armored with vicious blades, axes, and hammers. Few of these Dragokin were armed with mystical bows and deadly daggers. Though each of these Warriors varied between their mystical armor and weaponry, they were not the ones I truly was intrigued with.

The truly frightening of the bunch were but only two of the nearby Dragokin. They were terribly similar to the shadow-like being that silenced the enemy Dwarf with such ease. These Dragokin had a smoky aura that slithered in their paths, and unlike the other Warriors nearby, it seemed they were not much for words. Although the other Warriors were not forces to be reckoned with, there was this terrifying impression that emitted from these elder Dragokin Warriors.

By this point, there was still no word of how long this trail we were enduring would last. It seemed to be endless, as if we would chase the moon through an eternity of night, and the sun through never ceasing days. Mother did not falter. Her own feelings and heart were concerned, but there was this strength I could feel beating from her chest. However, I could sense her own worry grew deeper and more immense. That her sturdy yet troubling heart would never find peace within itself again.

We could vaguely hear the whispering chatter within the crowds. Words of concern, pain, and fear. Their questioning statements so soft and subtle that if not closely listening, the winds would carry them off without finding ears:

"Why has war been called upon us?"
"Where are we to find new lives?"
"How could such events unravel in the blink of an eye?"

The Warriors, though, did not appreciate the solitude of such a silence we were confined within. They engaged in rowdy conversation with one another as if there were not a worry in the world. As if such intense pressure and uncertainty were all but abnormal.

As the Warriors were chattering about, there was but one to approach Mother. "M'Lady, it seems our people seek words brought forth by someone much wiser than our troops leading the retreat," the Dragokin with a massive mystical bow brought to her attention.

"**Talonux**, the War Chief himself, appointed this section to protect and guide the retreat. I am sure our people have faith in **our** protection," a brawny Dragokin with the massive, serrated blade chuckled as he leaned upon Talonux's shoulder.

"*Yes,* **Bromyx,** *we can simply pull our people from the pits of battle and expect them to be sure our path is aflame,*" Talonux sarcastically replied as he brushed Bromyx from his shoulder.

"**Bah**, the 2nd Command is of high prestige. No words are needed in our presence." Bromyx argued.

"**Commanders**, do not bicker like boys in the school yards. Do not forget I watched as you all grew up. Since you were but my Dragons age. Talonux means no offense from his words, he speaks the truth. As Shield Maiden **I** must comfort our people," Mother responded. It seemed all the nearby Warriors blushed with embarrassment from Mother's words.

In perfect synchronization, the nearby Commanders replied, "*Yes M'Lady.*"

"Now, please, Talonux, send word to the lead of this pack that when an opening becomes available, I would like to speak to our people," Mother replied with a sense of purpose in her voice.

"Your words are my command, M'Lady," Talonux stopped momentarily to salute Mother, "**Scout Manoryx**, carry out your Shield Maiden's orders!" he continued over his shoulder to the pack of Warriors that trailed us.

    A Dragokin that was equipped like that of Talonux stopped immediately in his tracks. His green hood lifted while revealing a rough, tanned hat pointed at the tip. His emerald eyes luminated brightly as energies flickered in his skin. Without a word, I witnessed him harnessing his own swirled aura.

    He seemed concentrated, steadily positioned with one hand behind his back, while the other positioned in front of him. A gleaming green aura had begun whirling around him, but no one else took notice to this. Then, a surge of energy burst from his very soul, and he dashed towards to the front of the retreating masses with utmost haste.

    I was truly left in astonishment from what just had happened, and it seemed no one else shared those feelings. My eyes widened to such a display of physical speed. This had to be that of the power Bromyx held highly within his claims. I could only imagine that the combined strength of these Warriors would become truly overwhelming for me to bear witness.

In the distance, along the ridgelines of the mountains, I noticed more Warriors. They were strategically placed, standing watch over this caravan of the innocent. Compared to the exceptionally large amount of our retreating masses, the Warriors were vastly outnumbered, but even so, they watched carefully over the caravan from all angles. The innocent were shielded within a fine, yet highly lethal line of brutal beings.

From the rear of our retreating masses, I was soon to notice a few Dragokin Warriors rushing toward us. They left a dusted trail behind their tracks. It did not seem as if they were panicked, just moving with sensible purpose. Soon, all the Commanders that trailed Mother took notice to this as well. One by one they formed a defensive perimeter around Mother.

As the Warriors were advancing passed the crowds, we could notice words being expressed, accompanied by hand gestures. We could only assume that they were attempting to avoid widespread panic of their approach. There was but only one Scout, and two heavily armored Dragokin approaching us. From such a distance their entirety could only vaguely be detailed. As they drew closer, the Commanders still scanned from horizon to horizon, and signaled the distant Warriors, tightening their barrier around Mother.

"M'Lady, we have got friendlies approaching from the rear," the burley Dragokin with two vicious axes muttered as he took up a defensive posture.

Mother stopped while the remaining retreating masses continued, "If not words from my Chief, **I will but lash them myself**." Every Commander looked to Mother with concern. I could feel their hearts drop as if they believed Mother to be cruel. Being so close to her heart, I could feel the wit in her words, "Have you all lost humor along this trail? **Drop your stances** and allow your men in, **freely**," Mother pacified.

The Commanders were quick to break from their defensive posture around Mother, and the Warriors were soon to approach us. As the Warriors were attempting to find their breath they collapsed to their knees from exhaustion, then Mother erupted, "**Men**, your Commanders said if you do not yield words from the War Chief, you might as well turn now and return to where you came from, *before lashings emerge*."

Fear was struck in the eyes of the breathless Warriors that approached, and Bromyx questioned as he reached towards his troops with concern, "**But**, *M'Lady*...."

"Oh, find your hearts placed back within your chests. I but only humor you." Mother chuckled, "Now young Warriors, find your breath and when ready, **speak**."

"Shield Maiden, we do in fact bring words from the War Chief and frontlines," the Scout panted as a mystical shell shattered from around his being, exposing a more horrifying scene.

"**Bring forth water for these men immediately!**" Mother ordered while hastily pacing forward.

The Commanders handed over their own jugs of water for the exhausted Warriors. As they were replenishing, restoring their lost strength, and finding breath within their chest, Mother approached the Scout. She placed me on the ground next to her and I sat to observe. She began noticing the injuries this Scout had suffered. Such severe wounds pooled concerning amounts of blood within his garbs and puddled beneath his still position.

"Young Scout, **your injuries**?! Such severity should not be pushed as you have just done!" Mother gasped as she continued, "Such matters could not have been of concern M'Lady, we amongst the many were but the only ones to stand as the others were severely injured among the 1st Command. To be ordered with such a task, we thought fit enough to secure its path," the Scout mustered through his fatigued and blood spurting breath.

"Quiet now young Scout, before you speak any further." Mother was concerned as she pulled him from the ground and carefully leaned him forward.

Mother softly grabbed the Scouts face. Her eyes shined brightly as his own became locked within such an angelic aura. Then, a bright green aura with golden sparks flickered from Mothers hands and she whispered, *"**Breath of Talontuin**!"*

As Mother was gently holding onto this young and exhausted Scout, some of the Commanders stepped back in subtle fear. It was as if Mother's power stirred question in their hearts. Even though it was such a subtle action, I too sensed the immense surge of energies that emitted from Mother's being.

The Scout's posture began to stiffen slightly, but it seemed he was consumed with gracious peace within this moment. The bright green aura and golden sparks from Mothers hands began absorbing into his very being. Any detail of physical exhaustion or battle etched gashes seemed to disappear from existence.

Afterwards, Mother released her grip from around the Scout's face. As the green aura and golden sparks began to fully absorb into him, he gasped snappishly, and his eyes widened whilst momentarily flickering a mirrored aura such as Mother's eyes.

I could not help but to observe the fearful, yet curious astonishment found within the Commanders eyes. I was too attempting to decipher what had just happened. I crawled over to Mother while pulling myself onto her for balance.

The Commanders surely had a better understanding, but there was not joy within their hearts from witnessing this. Some clenched onto their weapons. Some were beginning to grow fearful whilst taking a step back. As if they knew of Mother's powers but did not fully grasp its full potential.

"**M'Lady**, *thank you!*" the Scout said softly with a rejuvenated tone.

"No, thank you, young Scout. Now, what words do you bring for us?" Mother cheerfully replied.

"The War Chief, Charmortus, wishes to advise this caravan of their own successful retreat. He has yet to give a time frame, as they are still battling the opposing forces whilst furthering from the villages, but the remaining masses of our armies and the remaining crowds of the villages will nonetheless be accompanying us. Also, the War Chief warns that this enemy seems to seek more than the mere possession of our lands," the Scout ended as he began finding his own ground.

"Your words do bring forth joy within my heart young Scout, seek a Medicus for you and your men. Rest your bodies and minds. Until further notice, your orders are to recover," Mother said as she pulled me from my swaying legs and gripped me to her hip.

"Shield Maiden." The Scout bowed before Mother and began assisting his brethren to their own feet.

As the Warriors broke from our position, Mother's gaze wandered the crowds. This time, her gaze was more focused, searching rather than observing. As Mother continued to glare around, the Commanders were still left in awe from what they just witnessed.

"Set your minds to ease Commanders, you have yet to experience why I was bestowed the title Shield Maiden." Mother broke the Commanders whispering words as she continued to scan the crowds.

"M'Lady, you have just revealed to not only us standing here, but to those around, that our Shield Maidens strength alone could possibly overcome even the force of Warriors that surround us," one of the haunting Dragokin with the shadowed aura broke through his own silence.

"The prophecy is unveiling Nemmonis, there is no need for any of our powers to be sheathed any longer," the other elder Dragokin with the dreadful aura confessed.

"**Overmortus**, we have all known the Shadows but clench on the edge of sanity with mere threads, but explain to us why you are not questioning the Shield Maiden's ability to cast Ancient Forbidden Magic as the rest of us are?" the brute Commander spoke with hostility as he spun his vicious axes around.

Within the blink of an eye, Overmortus burst into a darkened mist and appeared behind the Commander that approached him with anger, *"Careful now,* **Scarborax**, *there is wisdom but only few sane minds can absorb."* Overmortus's shadow began to slither around Scarborax, and a vicious blade dripping vile ooze pressed against his neck.

Nemmonis was soon to disperse into his own blackened aura as well. Soon we were enclosed within his own darkness. Shadow-like figures began to emerge from the smokey mist around us, each displaying their own disturbing appearance. They slowly paced around as a tension began to stir within the air around us.

These actions being taken caused confusion between the Commanders and the Warriors that followed. Aura illuminating weapons were beginning to draw, and fellow Dragokin were beginning to take up stances against one another. Even my own mind began to fill with a madness that I have never experienced. My body was tense and there was a sudden explosive rage. I began to abruptly scratch around and forcibly struggle against Mothers protective grasp.

Each Warrior began to harness their own magical energies, their eyes beginning to glow, and their minds just as clouded as mine. Though hard for me to focus on everything happening, it seemed chaos would soon unleash, and blood shed to occur. Every Warrior consumed in this darkness continued to steady their positions and ready their weapons. One false move within these moments could ignite ferocious battle.

As the shadow like figures began circling the Warriors, we could hear the villainous cackle echoing within our minds. As this sudden blood lust was continuing to consume me, I looked to Mother, and she stood unaffected.

Just before weapons could meet flesh, Mother begged, "**Overmortus, Nemmonis**, conceal your madness and release your grips. These men, our people, deserve an answer." "*Hmmmm.* **As you wish**, Quisvale," Overmortus responded with his deepened and cracked voice.

The darkened dome we were all confined within was soon to shatter. Overmortus and Nemmonis shaped back into their physical beings. With this, the sudden madness and rage we all were experiencing was slowly disappearing. The tension and hostility were also dispersing, as the shadow-like beings seeped back into the grounds we stood upon.

The Commanders and Warriors were shaking this power from their entire beings, but Mother seemed to not have been affected at all. Then, Mother noticed Scarborax still bore rage within his eyes. Mother carefully walked towards him as his own power and magical aura was beginning to rise.

Mother placed her hands upon his vicious axes, "Scarborax, please, collect your breath and I shall ease your minds." As Mother spoke these words, her eyes were filled with a divine light.

Scarborax looked to Mother, and then back to Overmortus and Nemmonis. The two Shadows were menacingly laughing as he was attempting to find his peace again. Even with hesitation heavy on his heart, and rage burning through his veins, the Commander slammed his axes into their holsters.

"**My apologies**, M'Lady, but with all that is happening, our minds are beginning to break and question even the fabric of nature," Scarborax huffed as he kneeled before Mother.

"No need for sincerity, it is **I** that should apologize. Upon this caravan reaching a halt, I will speak to our people. I will unveil the truth," Mother confessed while pulling Scarborax back to his feet.

Even though there was almost a battle between our own Warriors and Commanders, it seemed the retreating masses took no notice of such hostility among us. Within those moments, which seemed to only be an instant, our position at the end of the formation proved that more time had passed. The last few crowds of our people were catching up with the masses as we stood there.

"Let us find the lead of the formation and halt the retreat. We shall allow our people to rest, and I will bring light upon this troubling situation and reveal my true identity," Mother ordered as she began to follow the crowds.

As we were continuing with the crowds, the troubled, and now concerned, Commanders followed behind. They motioned for their nearby troops to continue as well. It was but only when the moon was nearing the horizon when our eyes witnessed the Scout Manoryx that was sent forward. With the same remarkable speed as before, he slid to a bowing stop before Mother.

"**M'Lady**, the Shadows are rallying our people upon the mountains plateau. The area is secure, and they await your command," Manoryx stated with not even a bead of sweat upon his face.

"Thank you Manoryx, let us find the lead so that we can ease troubled minds. Please, join me Commanders, leave your men to defend the rear of the retreat," Mother commanded. "Yes, M'Lady," the Commanders obliged.

    While the Commanders were addressing their Warriors, Mother began sprinting toward the top of the mountain. As she gripped me tightly against her body, she leaped onto a nearby boulder, and then-she lunged from the boulder, to completely ascend the skies. Her wings spread wide while dispersing a shimmering aura that followed.

    It was not long before the Commanders were following Mother's own actions. I gripped onto Mother's shoulder as we were flying through the skies with utmost speed. One by one I watched as the Commanders ascended the skies as well, their own auras bursting, as they were attempting to catch up.

CHAPTER FOUR
Ancient Secrets

I found there to be an intense feeling of relief, a sweet release from the continuous tension. A deepened sense of freedom as we soared high above the marching crowds. The sounds of Mother's wings fluttering widely, the precious wind brushing our cheeks as we glided above, there was peace found within the skies. Something I could sense would not last long. Something I am sure everyone yearned to feel. Though certainly not long enough to ease troubled minds.

Mother was making utmost haste to reach the top of the mountain. The Commanders were still worrisome of Mother, I could sense that within their pounding hearts. They were still yet proving not far behind our gaining position, fluttering about their own majestic wings. Our shadows were casting over the crowds of Dragokin continuing the retreat. I noticed few amongst the many, pointing towards us as we were flying high above.

Mother's remarkable strength allowed her to continue dashing towards the lead of our pack. She was leading fearsomely as everyone else below started to move with their own instilled purpose. Scattered atop the crown of the mountain, we could see little campfires spread throughout the plateau.

Dragokin were huddled near these fires whether for warmth, or to prepare what little food they had. Some were simply sitting around enjoying company with those they surrounded themselves with. No matter the case, I could feel Mother's heartwarming at the sight of our people being able to rest.

Further near the edge of the plateau was a darkened corner. There were but only shadows that stood watch over the next looming valley. Their own shadows seeping around them. This was where Mother directed her course and steadily descended toward. Her wings were now slowing their pace as we glided smoothly down.

The whispering winds carried Mother's stern tone over the opposing shoulder I was clenched firmly onto, "Commanders, see your visions true and we shall gather near that ridgeline where your Brothers stand watch. We shall all discuss this matter away from wandering or faltering ears."

"Yes, M'Lady!" the Commanders shouted, as their own auras were now too flickering, fading from being the nights light.

Mother spread her wings widely and began to thrust them slower, lowering her massive claws onto the mountains own hardened surface. With such extreme elegance, she landed whilst gusts of dirt and debris swirled in dusty clouds around us. She was gently cradling me tightly against her, covering my head against her shoulder as I watched her aura begin to dampen and flicker. Within the hasty blink of her even more so focused eyes, her warm and brightened aura dispersed into the gentle winds.

Mother paced towards the loosely formed group of decorated Warriors that were in snapping discussion. The moonlight was glaring from their blackened steel armor. Their words seemingly were attentively detailed depictions of the next luminating valley. Their remarks thoughtfully detailed about the path we had carved thus far into the ever so fresh surfaces of these mountains. Tiresome feet were but the only tools used to trench such a fresh path.

"If we are to keep from trails that have already been trodden, the retreat will take longer. But, if we are to… **M'Lady Quisvale**, welcome." A heavily armored and highly decorated Dragokin, with such a massive ancient detailed warhammer placed readily beside him, hailed confidently with his own bodies position tightening up.

Each of the brute and ceremoniously decorated Dragokin stopped whatever they were doing and halted their own scattered conversations. They burst from the ground if they were sitting. They all suddenly saluted Mother's graceful appearance. Mother just nodded at these Warriors and then turned to focus her sights on the trailing Commanders. They were now landing repeatedly behind her, kicking up their own gusts of dust as they landed.

Each Commander descended the skies and found their claws pressed against the hardened surface; they were soon to find their breaking paths placed by the opposing sides. Their own positions now nearest to the new group of Warriors. Those in which were finally forming their position.

All except Nemmonis and Overmortus, the darkened Shadows that have yet to be found far from Mothers sides. Their vile auras darkened as they whispered around in the thickening winds. The fewest of horrific Shadows, those that were lurking within this new group of Warriors, were sent screeching in the breeze and were soon to vanish from sight. They dispersed violently into a darkened mist and flowed with the passing breeze.

Now, I could feel a stiffened tension growing in the air between us. The two violently armed Warriors that stood by Mother had their hands clenched tightly onto the handles extended from their blood-stained blades.

Scarborax had begun whispering to the brute Dragokin. The one that initially greeted us displayed questionable anger, "**M'Lady**, is there *something* you wish to address?" As he broke from his still position and spoke his intensely expressed words, he was soon to ready his stance and slowly grasp his warhammer's leather wrapped handle.

"Engoryx, I would choose your actions wisely." Nemmonis chuckled darkly as his arms burst into a smoky mist. His sharpened shadows flailing around as imitating a wolf possessing many more than one tail.

"**Laws** are *laws*, **Nemmonis**. We know the shadows are protected under oath, but you cannot expect us to forget our duties, now, can you?" Engoryx replied as he draped his vicious warhammer across his broad and hardened shoulders.

"So, what do you think the War Chief would do about such matters in the circumstances we find ourselves between? How would he feel to find his beloved bound in chains?" Overmortus urged while he was painfully slouched over, gradually pulling a wicked shadow spear from the fabric of Nydeli's stone covered surface.

Before anything could suddenly and violently erupt between these Warriors, Mother carefully begged, "**Men**, *please*. Now is not the time for chaos amongst our own people. We have lost our homelands, Dragokin lives have been claimed, and we are set on a path with dwindling flames. I will answer all your questions, and rest assured, your troubling and questioning minds." She gracefully kneeled before the men, tears filling her eyes and casting from her dirt and charcoal covered cheeks.

It was at that moment I could sense a deep and passionate sympathy within the war beating hearts of ferocious beings. Nemmonis and Overmortus were the first to drop their violently aggressive forward stances. To follow, Engoryx hesitantly lowered his almighty warhammer's edge, carving the vicious serrated fangs deeply within the dirt below. He signaled for the remaining Warriors to drop their own fearfully instilled stances. As the breeze brushed over the edge of the mountain, there was complete stillness within the tense crowds.

"M'Lady Quisvale, **for now** I shall trust that your words prove true. Do not believe there to be a chance to evade the eyes we set upon you," Engoryx proclaimed while suddenly releasing the handle of his weapon.

Mother wiped the warm gushing tears from her heart felt eyes, and softly admitted through her sweet weeping voice, "*Of course.*"

Nemmonis and Overmortus floated to Mother's defeated sides, they gently pulled her to her own feet, and she tucked me tightly against her hips. The Warriors who now turned their backs against Mother, continued with their own chattering conversation.

I could not understand what was happening. There was but nothing Mother had done for me to understand why the Warriors turned so quickly against her. So, I just reached for Mother's face in desperate attempts to comfort her. When Mother's-soaked eyes finally met mine, it was as if everything around us stopped within the sands of time. We were lost within that heart warmed moment. As the pools of tears began to settle within her slithering silver eyes, one last tear rolled down her charcoal etched cheeks, splashing against my scarless flesh. Mother just smiled and hugged me snugly.

"Quisvale, shall we rally our people closer?" Nemmonis questioned as it seemed he had already been gathering his own energies.

"**Yes**, *please*, **they all deserve an answer**." Mother trembled as she broke from my focused attention and curiously following eyes.

Both Overmortus and Nemmonis kneeled before Mother's strengthening presence and burst into ghastly shadows. They slowly stood and turned, cracking, and popping from her position. They paced towards the gathering crowds of our people. A darkened aura began to emit from the stones below them. Unhurriedly, the image of an ancient symbol appeared, glowing deeply. They both raised their hands, shaking slowly as they extended higher.

I could now see more ghostly figures seeping from the grounds within the crowds. As they emerged, it seemed they were contacting the faltering masses. Soon, everyone started to hastily find their own paths towards us. By the masses, every Dragokin within the numbers of our retreat, were now approaching Mother's settling position. Even as distant as they all were, I could still witness the confusion and exhaustion painted across their faces.

As they continued to patiently gather around Mothers leading position, she stood stoically upon an overlooking boulder. Mother placed me on the ground while helping me balance my own stance. As I fell forward, quickly I clasped onto Mother's leg. Her claws uncovered the fabrics that were wrapped tightly, concealing my wings. The moment my bare bone wings were exposed, I could hear the fearsome gasping within the gathering crowds.

Then, as I was clenched so tightly, my own legs waving around, Mother took up her own balanced stance while being consumed in a brightly reddened and gold sparking aura. An impeccable silver light escaped and was now swirling abruptly around Mother's very being. Red and golden sparks began to vastly spurt from her body. Her wings spread widely as they seemed to begin harnessing brightly shaded orbed energies from Nydeli herself.

There were now intense emotions swelling in all those around. The Warriors along the mountains edge were soon to also find their trembling positions nearest Mother. Though their faces painted confidence, in their hearts I could sense a rising fear. They took up a more defensive stance as Mother's power was intensifying. I clumsily fell from being positioned steadily against Mother's leg. I was now sitting, as the gusts of her power splashed from her heart and soul.

Scarborax attempted to break from the vicious line of Warriors, but Engoryx's hand hastily stopped him from coming any closer. I watched as the remaining Warriors were too expressing that in which Scarborax was filled with. But, of all the hostile positioned Warriors, it was Engoryx's own heavy heart that I felt the only bit of faith within.

Mother began waving her hands elegantly, swaying them in distinct patterns, flowing with the very breeze that tenderly grazed our flesh and scales. She then tightly clasped her hands together and she again burst with unremarkable power. There was an immense shimmering mist that swirled violently around us, concealing Mother and I within its mystical presence. The moment that all her illuminating auras and flickering energies had settled and drifted off into the winds, the eyes of all those around begun widely shaking upon us.

Mother's aura had finally faded from flashing finely in our eyes, and now my own eyes truly witnessed that in which I have never seen. It was as if she stood stoically above me casting a completely different shadow. Mother's wings, her scales, her very being, transformed. Now, Mother's wings were just as mine, bare bones.

Her aged wings bore deepened etchings of war. Her left wing seemed to have been severely maimed as well, as if a blade had sliced through it. Mother's scales and flesh bore more severe engravings of battle. Also, within Mother's eyes, there was a deepened sense of pain, few blackened tears now dribbled down her once soft cheeks.

"**Citizens of Bundok ng Dragon, I, Quisvale Gray-Flame**, Shield Maiden of these lands now reveal myself entirely as the Bearer of Light, the Forgotten Daughter, **a Lost Soul**." Mother brokenly wept through her trembling lips, "**My Father, Draxperil the Forsaken.**"

As Mothers words echoed over the frightfully rowdy crowds, a deepened fear swept heavily towards us. Dragokin began to slowly pace backwards, as if they intended a new retreat. It seemed those shaking within their steps wanted to get as far from Mother as they could. The Shadows within the shoving crowds were doing their best job to keep everyone calm and maintained. We both could sense the chattering within the crowds were of doubt, of lost hope, of disgust.

Then, his mighty Warhammer tapped against the boulder, silencing all those around, stopping everyone within their tracks, Engoryx stood with solidarity in his heart next to Mother, "**Though we fear what has been brought into the light, use your own hearts to feel that of your Shield Maidens**! For I, myself *questioned*, yet I sense no intentions of The Forsaken within her. Still, her heart beats as the loving and fearless Shield Maiden we have grown to, and willingly love."

Scarborax angrily burst with deadly rage from behind, "**Engoryx, have you lost your mind**!?"

Engoryx turned defensively around whilst stepping in front of Mother, "The exact opposite **Brother**, for centuries we have hunted those who practice the Ancient Arts, we now are being hunted as mere dogs ourselves. M'Lady Quisvale's own ability to harness such forbidden magic may yet prove useful in our retreat."

The rage was still building deeply within Scarborax's heart. His approaching offense stopped dead in their tracks. He was clenching his ferociously sharpened axes tightly. The remaining Warriors began sheathing their own drawn weapons, and slowly joined nearest Engoryx's position.

Scarborax's deeply reddened aura continued to grow vastly intense. Then, he turned his back on the defensive line positioned in front of Mother. Without words, he powerfully dove over the edge of the mountain in complete disgust.

Mother quickly broke through the defenses around her, pushing towards the edge to follow Scarborax, but Engoryx respectfully stopped her,

"Allow him to gather his thoughts M'Lady. His past fuels the rage for forbidden magic, **you know this** better than anyone. We are still worrisome of this development, but we believe in our hearts that you are still the Shield Maiden that has never led us astray."

Mothers quivering eyes wandered and found Engoryx's. She just nodded in defeated agreement. I could sense within her heart that she was desperately seeking such comfort to arise from all those around. That her revealing herself to the already troubled hearts within the crowds, she has possibly stained her once respected image within their eyes. That her own upbringing and origins may cause our people to lose complete faith in her words.

Engoryx dropped his ancient Warhammer and then cautiously kneeled next to me,

"And I see that you too have Forsaken blood running through your veins, **don't you**, *young one*? To think I have seen it all." Engoryx chuckled as he picked me up carefully, "**Commanders**, find that our people ease their troubled minds, I have a feeling our lady-yields more words."

All the Commanders that stood upon that boulder were soon to drop their defensive stances. They saluted Engoryx and suddenly leapt from the overlook we stood upon. They began dispersing within the crowds, assisting the Shadows with civilized crowd control. I witnessed as they skillfully controlled the panic that was emerging from Mothers words alone. I still could sense hesitation, and fear within their hearts, as they began to regain their positions nearest Mother.

There were but few groups that I witnessed making their ways through the crowds hastily, confidently gaining positions nearest to Mother. As it seemed, they truly sought more of Mothers words. That even though most were now fearful of her, there stood but few who's faith was not completely shattered.

"**My people, my tribe, my kin, and pack**. My heart trembles for the deceit I have displayed. To keep such a secret from those I have fought with, from those I have feasted with, from those I have drank and howled at the moons with. It was but to earn your love and confidence without the haunting of my own past shadowing your thoughts. My heart does not pump vile blood, my mind does not yield treacherous intentions, my soul does not seek the path of the Forsaken. Please, find that confidence and love you have yielded for me once before, and allow me to lead our pack until our War Chief, the remainder of our Kin, the Warriors that have continued to stand and fight, find themselves by our sides once again." Mother had confidently preached over the silence of the crowds.

As Mother's echoing voice began to fade, Engoryx shifted me into Mother's nurturing grips. She held me tightly against her hip, both our wings casting thickened shadows across the surface of these lands. I grew cheerful within her arms and began to giggle uncontrollably as she embraced me ever so lovingly.

My little wings were flapping with the purest joy, my sharpened claws grabbing at her delicate face, my feet wiggling about as my claws scratched against her. The tears in Mother's eyes had begun to settle, the continuous pools now drying. Her own heart was now fluttering while finding such much-needed joy.

Mother's sights broke from my own unconditional glance as she noticed the crowds were still trembling in silence. Then, from the front of the crowds, we witnessed a group of Dragokin kneel before us. Mother gasped with a burst of joy, throwing one hand against her quivering lips. The warmest of love pouring from her throbbing heart. Then, another group within the front of the crowds bowed before us.

One by one, as a wave, Dragokin were kneeling before Mother. Their own hearts now regaining the almost lost love for her. There but stood only one within the masses, but we could sense their intended respect towards Mother. Her silver-streaked eyes filled with warmed tears once again, this time I knew they were tears of joy.

"**Now**, let us prepare for our journey onward. Through the night we shall find the comfort of concealment, ready yourselves and place your faith back within." Engoryx cheered as he raised his almighty warhammer, presenting honor amongst the crowds, "**M'Lady Quisvale!**" as he too bowed before Mother, ceremoniously holding his weapon in front of him.

With this newly restored faith bursting from the hearts within all those around, the weakening trouble that weighed Mother's heart was now peacefully lifted. Engoryx paced from the overlook and signaled for the Commanders to return to their position at the edge of the mountain. As they began breaking from the crowds and pacing towards us, Engoryx welcomed Mother and the Shadows along the edge of the mountain as well. As the Commanders regained their positions from before, the planning for our continued retreat burst with conversation.

"Now that we have set aside any clouded judgement, let us continue with M'Lady Quisvale among our ranks," Engoryx stated as he sat along the chipping edge.

Mother was soon to join him, placing my own legs over the avalanching edge and collapsing beside me on her knees, *"Thank you* Engoryx. For I swear that I am still the Dragokin, the Shield Maiden of our pack, that you have all trusted and loved for so long."

The moon was nearing its darkened horizon as plans for the retreat continued to unveil. I was not paying much attention towards their meticulous words, as I was growing overwhelmingly tiresome. Mother took notice to my sleepy gaze, and she pulled me towards her plush legs. She began to swaddle me within cloths, and hum ever so softly.

As I was battling this tiresome feeling, Mother placed her warm cheek upon mine and began swaying me in her arms. It seemed such sweet a song Mother hummed, and it began to uplift the hearts of those within earshot. Within moments of such beautiful serenity, I was soon to drift from consciousness and become silently seduced into the dream realm.

CHAPTER FIVE
ONCE A SHIELD MAIDEN, ALWAYS A SHIELD MAIDEN

My tiresome eyes began to hastily twitch. I could feel the morning's chilled breeze sweeping against my grimy cheeks. I jostled within the tightened grip of Mother's arms; I could feel her loving embrace tightening me against her. I did not wish to wake just yet, for within this moment I had found profound comfort within a heartwarming clasp. My hands began to slide over my awakening eyes, to shade the light that was attempting to breach them.

The thundering sound of marching began to pique my waking interest, the echoing chatter of the crowds. The brief orders commanded from one Warrior to the next. Such sounds would prove to my ears that we were no longer at the mountaintop encampment. That we were once again carving visibly witnessed paths deeper upon the mountains beaten surface. Continuing towards the distant horizon leading absent the paths of our relentless enemies.

My body craved more deepened rest, but my rising mind grew briskly curious. Slowly my eyes cracked the sluggish seal of slumber, witnessing the days new brightening and illustrious rising sun. Reddened rays of sunshine were rapidly scattering through the virgin skies, revealing a smooth sapphire canvas, painted with auburn streaks. As my eyes began to feel less weighted, Mother glanced down at me and wiped my settling eyes.

"Rise and shine my Dragon!" Mother suddenly cheered as she snuggled her face against mine.

From such a moment realized, I knew there would be no returning back within the dream realm. That surely, I would undeniably succumb to unconsciousness when my body and mind needed. As I began to stretch and find my head rested upon Mother's shoulder, my glance began swaying to witness the rallying crowds. Focusing my attention on the passing masses, I could feel their guilty eyes peaking over towards us. As if they did not wish to stare for too long, but their own curiosity needed to be satisfied.

This was when I truly realized we were different from everyone within the crowds. Though not every Dragokin within the masses appeared the same, it was their own wings that made me wonder. Both Mother and I had bare skeletal wings, lacking leathery skin. Our scales darkened, absent of a shimmering glare. The rest of our people, our pack that followed, had gleamy scales varying different shades of the spectrum and grime smeared flesh that covered their wings.

Mother stood vigilant watch over the caravan as thousands of Dragokin passed us. Not even one other Dragokin shared the same traits as us. My head rested upon Mother's curvy shoulder and my eyes continued searching. Deep within my heart I was yearning to learn the very essence of being, longing to understand the principles of life.

"Was this truly what stirred fear into their hearts?"
"The apparent substantial alteration between them and us?"
"How could such a difference express such distress amongst them?"

My focus now set towards Mother as I realized she was not only standing careful watch. She too was curiously examining the scattered crowds. Her eyes piercing through, carefully depicting our surroundings. Suddenly, a burst of joyous excitement erupted from Mother.

Breaking from our still position, she began to cheerfully hustle through the parting crowds. Dragokin would stop in their tracks or respectfully step aside as Mother was pacing through. I could still sense a subtle fear within them. I could still sense their questioning hearts.

This subtle untrust still vibrating within our people did not seem to break Mother's heart anymore. It seemed she understood their sprouting feelings much better than I could, that there wielded an established reasoning for their newly developed feelings towards her.

"**Vodish**! I have been searching for you!" Mother ecstatically erupted through the bustling crowds.

As Mother continued forward, I noticed a brute figure slouched within the hordes. This had to have been whom Mother desperately called for. Everyone else around continued furthering the trail around us, whereas this burly individual stood still as Mother beckoned. I began to grow intrigued with this brawny individual. As he revealed his position and turned towards us, it seemed we were not the only beings that were uniquely different.

"*Ahhhh...* **Quisvale**... Your energies are not easily mistaken. You have enflamed curiosity in this old Orcs soul." Vodish replied as we finally approached.

Vodish pulled the ragged hood that concealed his true appearance. He was not that of Dragokin blood. Absent of monstrous wings. No hardened scales to cover parts of his body. Of the thousands, he was of his own. This man's voice sounded familiar to that of the Shadows. Dark and cracked. The natural aura which emitted from his being was that of more friendly grasp than that of the Shadows. It was quite welcoming. Soothing. Warm.

Beneath the tattered and heavy robes, shined ancient armor of historical wars. His gray beard was braided and bound with iron rings. He carried with him a massive, chained tome and a withered old staff. Within the emeralds that were his eyes, swirled immaculate darkened shades of green. Staring into his eyes felt like looking over a meadow of wild grasses. There was peace found within, and around this man. His skin was a brightened green just as his eyes were, and two stained ivory teeth towered from his mouth.

Next to this elderly man followed a ferocious monstrosity, that so obediently accompanied his side. Its razor claws and sharpened talons seemed deadly to the point. Its chipped fangs serrated the edges of its mouth. It had a long powerful tail that swept the dirt beneath. Hardened scales covered this creature's body, just like that of our own. This magnificent beast stood just as tall as Mother and walked upon two legs.

As ferocious as this creature looked, its own aura matched that of the elder mans. Welcoming, and too anciently decorated. There were mystical chains, jeweled with emeralds, that dangled from its head. There was also a dusty mount draped upon its back, covered with burlap sacks that were stuffed to the brim with damaged scrolls.

"Vodish, would you and Sorth care to join me aside from the crowds?" Mother asked, while tenderly wrapping her arm around his.

"I can see there is much to discuss, Quisvale." Vodish calmly claimed as we turned together, "Your true identity revealed can only mean one thing."

Mother's grip remained locked onto Vodish as we retraced our steps to the side of the retreating masses. The vicious appearing creature whom Mother addressed as Sorth followed warily close as we unhurriedly made our way out of the crowds. Without intense examination, I noticed there was a very subtle aura connected between Vodish and the prehistoric beast that followed. If not paying close attention I would have surely missed such an existence. A tether, although faint, shimmered between the gap they made.

We finally pulled from the crowds retreating trail as Mother was taking to Vodish's own pace. There was a collection of boulders nearby that Mother guided us toward. Vodish began positioning himself on a flattened stone, and there was a breath of relief roughly exerted. Shortly afterwards, Sorth found itself nestling into the dirt beside Vodish. Mother too rested next to Vodish on both knees and rested her head against his brawny legs.

"Vodish, I cannot help but to fear it was my fault we are all being hunted…" Mother concerned with trembling tears building within her concerning eyes.

"Oh child, there is more to life than one's past. Though Forsaken blood courses through your veins, you cannot carry the weight of assumption on your shoulders. There are no clear answers to life, young one." Vodish chuckled as his arms stretched behind him and he watched the azure skies.

"*Yes, but why must such devastation be brought upon us?*" Mother pleaded as her warm tears continued pooling and trailing down her soft cheeks.

"Even us Druids are unable to answer all the questions of life. We but fill the tomes and pass the torch. Life is an ever-changing entity that will forever present questions. So, our lives should be dedicated to seeking out those answers, and to always expect more questions. To think we know it all, is to know nothing at all, young Quisvale." Vodish explained as he closed his eyes and leaned further back.

Mother curled and cradled me within her arms, her eyes were deeply invested into mine, "*I suppose your right Vodish...*"

We stayed rested upon those boulders for quite some time as our kin continued to pass. As I was peeking around, I could feel the exhaustion within all those who continued the trail. Not one of us slept without restlessness. We sat in silence as our pack tirelessly pushed through the vigorous mountains. Mother was swaying me in her arms as she hummed a beautiful tune. All of those within earshot of such a serenading song were showered with calmness.

Vodish broke the silence that was settled between us, "Your love is an overwhelming one to accept, so have faith that your people still believe in you. It is but your heart they sense, so prove even the Forsaken can bear true light."

After Vodish spoke, he shook his companion from the temporary peace found within its soundless slumber. Mother was too stretching from the dirt and finding her own ground. As it seemed we were preparing for departure, a darkened cloud began to emerge from the mountain's surface.

Sorth was quick to take a defensive posture in front of Vodish's own unenthusiastic positioning. It seemed Vodish did not feel threatened, nor did Mother. This cloud began to shape into a Dragokin, and it seemed to be a Warrior of the Shadows, one that I have never seen before.

"M'Lady Quisvale," her haunting voice began to crackle, "Nemmonis sends word that requests you at the lead of the pack."

As this vile Dragokin bowed, Mother snappishly questioned, "**What is it?**"

As the sadistically cloaked Dragokin became fully formed, Sorth began to violently screech and snarl towards her. The haunting shadow returned her own menacing hiss and then obliged Mother,

"There seems to stand a force that will sway our path. He seeks your guidance." In the blink of an eye, she burst into a darkened mist, and swiftly vanished through the winds.

"Vodish, care to accompany me? I would feel comforted with your familiar soul in my presence." Mother begged as she began fastening me tightly against her hip.

"Of course, Quisvale, once your Guide, always your Guide. Sorth needs to stretch her legs anyways," he steadily agreed while calming his troubled companion.

Once Mother was finished tightening me against her body, she stretched her illustrious wings widely, and slowly restored her balance. I whole-heartedly believed we were now prepared entirely for the purpose of travel. Then, I witnessed a burst of youth emerge from this visibly elderly man.

As he dusted off the mount on his companion, he stretched, unleashing blaring waves of snaps and crackles. With no assistance and considerable speed, he swung stoically on top of the mount saddled to his faithful steed.

"Do not let this old Raptors age fool you Quisvale, she has not yet seen her prime stage of life," Vodish said while patting the smooth olive scales covering Sorth's neck.

"*It is a race then,*" Mother chuckled.

Mother finished adjusting herself, positioning for travel, and Vodish clacked his heels against Sorth's sides, and she began galloping with remarkable speed. Mother was soon to follow suit and began sprinting. While clenching me tightly against her, Mother began leaping forward with significant distance. With each formidable stride she was flapping her powerful wings. Then, a burst of energy flowed through Mother and her wings began to glow. Between her bare skeletal wings, shimmered sheets of magical beams that were of an iridescent essence.

Before the winds lifted us, and we completely ascended from the ground, we were heel to heel with Vodish and Sorth. The moment Mother glided into a dashing flight path, and sent vicious clouds of gust around us, I felt that this race was finished before it truly started. That is when I noticed a humorous look upon Vodish's blemished and wrinkled face.

He began to distinctly wave his arms around in concentrated patterns, focusing the energies that pulsed from his life force. He bled his very heart and soul directly into Sorth. Then, a green energy flickered within Sorth and her entire being bulged with a glistening aura.

Mother thrusted her wings hastily, while Vodish and Sorth began to trail her path. It seemed so effortless for them. As if they were but toying with Mother. They were soon to find themselves by our side again, and Mother looked over with her own witty smile. It seemed Mother was soon to become outmatched. With one more click of his heels, Vodish and Sorth were now leaving us in their own thickening cloud of dust.

There was joy found within this friendly bout of speed. As if they were but chasing one another with no other cares surrounding us. Even with Vodish and Sorth's gaining position, I sensed there was hesitation in their true untamed strength. That this was but only for show and not true competition.

Unfortunately, it was not long before their festive hearts became stern. We noticed the retreating masses were forced into an abrupt halt. The Dragokin cautiously spread throughout the mountainside. It seemed as if they were all within a defensive posture as well. Vodish began to dismount Sorth, as they too had stopped abruptly within their tracks. Mother began to slow her own flight and she readied us for landing. While her wings were thrusting slowly, she carefully landed upon the ground.

"There is true **fear** to sense here, Quisvale," Vodish worried as he was tightening his belongings to the saddle equipped onto Sorth. "**Yes**, I too sense this." Mother's joy was diminished as she continued approaching.

Within our sights, we now witnessed the Commanders crouched, peeking over boulders, trading scattering words, and becoming exceedingly tense. Taking utmost caution while finding closer position to their displayed concern, we all warily crouched as we paced into the group of bickering Commanders.

As we drew closer, two recognizable blackened clouds began to emerge next to Mother. "M'Lady Quisvale," Both Nemmonis and Overmortus greeted Mother as their beings became solidified.

    I could feel a growing hostility emitting from behind us, as it seemed Vodish and Sorth thoughtlessly stopped following near our side. He was still holding Sorth's head down, clenching together her clattering jaws. I could feel she wanted to burst, as she had savagely displayed before within the glooming presence of the Shadows. There were visible energies tethering between Vodish and Sorth, vaguely appearing as luminescent chains. Then, as Vodish continued to fill Sorth with his very aura, it seemed the Raptor was guided gently into a sudden slumber.

"Next time, a warning would be appreciated." Vodish quietly argued as he grabbed his weather staff and found his position near Mother again. "Your pet Raptor lacks proper training, *Vodish*," Nemmonis responded with his own disgust. "*Please*, **not now**," Mother begged.

The Commanders were all formed in a circle around a weakening aura. We discovered that the painful aura belonged to Scarborax, the Dragokin that had previously displayed such appalled rage towards Mother. Although he was found to be back within their ranks, he seemed to be critically injured. Medicus Dragokin were tending to his wounds, but his deepened gashes of battle seemed to be too severe to treat, despite their best efforts. I could sense his heart weakening. His breaths becoming lesser. His soul slowly fading.

Mother was quick to rush over as her heart began to shatter, "**Scarborax**?! **What happened**?!" her eyes widened, and glistening tears formed. Her own aura began to flicker, and her words were desperately shaking.

"*No, M'Lady, do not waste your powers... do not waste your powers on me...*" Scarborax mustered through thickened blood bursting from his mouth. "**Do not be a fool**, allow me to..." Mother gasped before Scarborax lowered her pattern drawing hands with his own trembling fingers.

"*I... am sorry... M'Lady... I allowed my life's task to blind me... to blind me of all that you have taught me... to fuel a clouded rage with misjudgment... I do not deserve your sorrow... Not after the way I behaved towards you...*" Scarborax confessed as he coughed up concerning amounts of blood.

"**No**... **No, I will not allow this!**" Mother broke through her burdening tears and her aura burst with red and gold sparks of energy. Mother's hands began to glow brightly, ancient symbols flashing within her flesh, and she gripped tightly onto Scarborax who was noticeably fading from this world, "**Please**, *this is not your fate!*"

As Mother began to exert all her energies into Scarborax, it seemed some of his injuries were beginning to seal. Everyone nearby stood in wonder as they were witnessing such. Mother continued to weep. That is when I noticed why her tears did not cease, Scarborax's injuries may have been healing, but his heart only continued to weaken. His soul continued to fade.

"*M'Lady.... Thank you....*" Scarborax whispered with his dying breath.

Even with Mother's miraculous powers, even with her undying efforts, such magic still was not enough to pull Scarborax from the edge of death. His being began to subtly glow, his own aura now flickering. Mother's tears cascaded down her face. She was the only one to weep. Everyone within eyesight just took a knee and bowed.

Mother began to hum a sweetened lullaby through her tears. Then, Scarborax's aura began to consume his physical being. His very soul and all that he was, now seeping into the passing winds. The sky seemed to begin to brighten. Just before Scarborax's body completely faded from this world, I witnessed the unfathomable.

Mother opened her eyes, exposing a divine light and raised her head. Mother began to find her ground, it seemed Scarborax's aura began to glow in the image of him. There were tears within his own eyes now. This ghostly image of Scarborax saluted Mother and then spread his wings widely. In that moment, it was as if we could hear the glorious roar of an approaching Dragon, and with such a divine presence above us, Scarborax's energies were pulled to the skies.

"*What... What happened*!?" Mother trembled with an unmistaken rage building from her heart and soul.

"*M'Lady*, Scarborax rushed from the mountaintop, he found himself blowing off steam in the village just beyond this peak. But..." Engoryx had started to explain before Mother paced quickly toward the crest of the mountain.

Mother's heart dropped upon unveiling the horrors of the village. Though we were distanced from the town, we could witness the chaos being unleashed. Enemies of our people were violently raiding the homes. Bringing forth havoc within their streets. We could faintly hear the desperate cries for help bursting from within. The feelings stirring in Mother were near my incapability of understanding. Love and hate. Life and death. Mother's own scales of life, of logical thinking, were becoming imbalanced.

"And we just stand here!?" Mother snapped while unfastening me from her hip. "We have pushed a Scout forward, and learned their numbers in Warriors outnumber our own, easily ten to one. Our mission is to guide the pack to the coast, **safely**. The Shadows are securing a path around and within concealment. We must not lose focus, M'Lady." Engoryx tried explaining.

"Vodish." Mother called. "Quisvale, you should already know the answer." Vodish replied while finding his place confidently next to Mother.

Mother continued to unfasten me from the saddle that stitched us together. Then, she handed me over to Vodish. Though this man was unfamiliar to me, his aura alone provided me with comfort. He cradled me in his arm carefully, and suddenly vines began to wrap around his arm. Resembling that of the saddle Mother had draped around her. He pulled me closer into his hardened muscles as the vines thickened. Even though my vision was obscured, I could still peek through the entangling vines.

"**I will not stand idly by any longer**! We will slice a path through our enemies! The War Chief and the remaining masses are soon to be with us, for now we will protect those who call for our help. Commanders assign your Lieutenants and have them lead the pack around. **Those who stand as Leaders will find themselves at my side!**" Mother ordered as her aura burst wildly and she began to hastily pace down the Mountain.

"**Overmortus**, gather a miniscule pack of hunters!" Nemmonis creaked as the two haunting shadows began to vanish from physical being.

Both Overmortus and Nemmonis burst into blackened mists. One of them trailing behind Mother, the other seeping into its position below. Shadowed spikes vaulted around on the mountain's surface. More and more Shadows were darkening the ground beneath us, and then they burst towards Mother. Slithering about. Their auras were beyond haunting in such vast numbers.

"**Argh**... **Lieutenants, you heard your Shield Maiden**! Prove your worth now young Officers!" Engoryx frustrated while arming himself with his massive warhammer and dashing towards Mother.

"**Finally, Brother**! Ease your mind, for we are about to fight alongside our Shield Maiden of tale! **There is honor within this moment!**" Bromyx chuckled as he slid a vicious blade through the dirt and charged to Mother's position.

"*Is this truly the route we have got to take?*" Talonux questioned as he too rushed forward whilst readying an arrow against his mystical bow.

"It has been years, Young One, since I have seen your Mother fight. I shall not miss how far my training has truly brought her." Vodish snickered as his own energies began to rise.

Vodish was soon to whistle, it was not very loud. I looked behind us to witness Sorth breaking from her slumber. As her eyes were snapping, adjusting to the light, her head swayed in our direction. It seemed she burst with joy as her eyes found us. She stood from her position and dashed towards us.

"Alright girl, if I am to bring you, you need to behave around those *vile Shadows*. Your focus will be set **elsewhere**," Vodish explained before we mounted Sorth. He clicked his heels against Sorth's sides, and onwards we were now trailing within this viciously trodden trail.

As we violently scurried down the mountain, each Commander near Mother's sides were harnessing their own energies, drawing their brutal weapons, and readying themselves for battle. Each of their auras glowed differently, from the way their energies flaunted in the winds, to the very colors they shimmered. Mother's wings spread widely, and her own silver aura began to consume her.

This was such an amazing sight to witness so closely. Mother's aura was significantly different than that of the Commanders. Her aura wisped around her body and armor began to form around her. Though transparent, I could see that her armor's details seemed ancient, from the times before we were now living. Then, Mother's sharpened claws began to split that of the world's fabric itself.

From one side, a finely double-edged sword guided smoothly into her grips. The sharpened edges seemed to be snapping chains, attempting to keep them within the darkness. From the other side, a darkened tower shield shaped as a dragon's head, began forming tightly to her arm. Mother tugged violently and broke the magical blade and shield from the ancient chains they were entangled within. The power I could feel from this entire group of Warriors, was not matched to that which I felt within Mother now. It seemed even the Commanders trembled in the presence of Mother's ever-growing and weighted power.

As we were approaching the smokey and enflamed town, the cries for help only grew disturbingly louder. Such devastation only continued to build a deadly rage within our offensively approaching pack. It did not seem we were taking a silent approach either. We treaded through the fields at the bottom of the mountain with no regard to concealment. Then, I could sense Mother was about to lose control of her very being.

Innocent women and children were being dragged from their homes, all collectively gathered in the center of the village. There were sounds of homes crumbling within towering flames, and the shattering of glass continued to screech. We could see the Dragokin men lined up on their knees before their terrified people. The villainous laughter from our enemies was stirring within the pain from the village.

Just as we were breaking the villages limits, we witnessed a distinguished stocky Dwarf soaked in the blood of our people, pacing in front of the chain bound men. It seemed an elder Dragokin was pleading for the lives of the others, desperately begging for their release. The Dwarf drug a vicious war axe behind him.

He burst with wicked joy and laughter as he swung this blood drenched weapon from the dirt and slashed through the neck of the unarmed and bound man. That action alone caused Mother to burst with endless rage. She charged directly into the mouth of the beast. War cries were breaking the balance of Nydeli.

CHAPTER SIX
FORSAKEN RAGE

Mother's echoing battle cry filled the air as we all began charging toward the village. The moment Mother's rage truly consumed her; our enemies became aware of our impending presence. From every corner of each enflamed building, bursting through the crumbling doors and plunging through the windows, more battle-hardened Dwarves were now rushing in our direction. There were sounds of weapons unsheathing, the trampling of the ground. Battle cries were now consuming the air and echoing through the rumbling fields.

Vodish was soon to dismount like a spearhead, and land in his own rose stance. I was wrapped within a woven shelter of entangling vines, winding wildly around his enormous arm. Vodish slammed the ground with intensely bursting energies pulsating through his other enormous palm, *"Halg's Dominion!"* he whispered in a deep and hollowed tone.

Orbs of green light suddenly emerged and began to swirl around us. Then, thickened vines had slowly begun emerging from Nydeli's surface. As these vines burst with growing density, they were rising from the very grounds, sprouting around, and harnessing as sculptures from the earth beneath us. Intertwining statues, taking the form of leafy beings.

These creatures rising from nature began taking physical forms like Vodish himself, although smaller. Made of nature's roots, and hardened with stones inside them, it was not hard to see why I was left in awe when they began to animate with their own physical and magical energies.

"**You will protect this young one at all costs**!" Vodish ordered as he placed me in the arms of one of these newly formed beasts.

My heart thumped as I watched the scene unfold. I was feeling extremely tense, being passed between others, carried further from Mother. But, with a seemingly instinctual and protective way, the vine covered entity held me against its chest, and I felt its limbs tighten around me. Its rough roots were scratching against my scales. I could smell the damp, cool earth that these beings emerged from, and I felt safe. By my count, there were six of them. One noticeably larger than the others. The leader, I thought. I watched and observed their unspoken communication. Knowing that although no words were spoken, a mutual understanding of sorts was bouncing between them.

While Vodish began to gather his own magical energies, I watched as these beings were now arming themselves with weapons that protruded through the emerald portals they emerged from. Long spiked wooden spears that dripped of a foul and vile ooze. The larger being ripped an ancient war axe from underneath the dirt and rocks. Sharpened brutally, it was as if Nydeli herself crafted these ferocious weapons to be at their divine disposal.

I focused my wandering sights and looked back over to Vodish. I noticed his hands were focused and pressed firmly against Sorth. He shouted in a bursting stance and strengthened tone, "**Halg's Strength**!"

Their auras were now merging in a violent gust, swirling around them both, whipping dust and pebbles in every direction. Then, a magical mist burst from their bodies and shimmered with the winds. There was a flash of blinding and brilliant light. As this magical mist had begun to settle, I witnessed that within the blink of an eye both Vodish and Sorth were heavily armored with ancient steel. Their physical forms seemed to now be bulging with undeniable strength, more so than I had sensed before.

Sorth screeched loudly as she began stretching and shaking this heavily ancient and tanned bark covered armor into place. Her own battle cry now echoing and rattling through the developing battlefield. Covered from head to toe in blackened ancient armor, spikes ridged the surface of the immaculate plates, and Sorth's eyes now shined brightly through the helmet protecting her head.

The ancient staff Vodish was wielding, was now shaping into a war forged, deadly spear. His armor too looked that of primordial times, heavy plates covered in mystical pelts. From the helmet down to his very boots, each piece of this ancient armor portrayed that of a mystical beast. As he finally finished readying himself, he was soon to glance over towards us.

"Ents! Find your place near Quisvale! Protect her and her child!" Vodish shouted as he too began to fearlessly charge into battle.

These Ents, the beings of nature, they did not speak. They but only charged towards Mother with astonishing speed. Vodish and Sorth were following closely beside us. There was an intense rage building within them, building within everyone around. We were soon to be found at Mothers side and I could now sense Mothers deepened and unending fury.

"READY YOURSELVES!" Mother ordered as we soon clashed violently with our enemies.

As I peeked around, just before the violent crash, I noticed each Warrior was now consumed in their own bloodlust. I was witnessing firsthand the rage of war with my own eyes. Magical auras were bursting from their beings, their battle cries forcing the veins in their necks to bulge, their eyes filled with a senseless and burning wrath.

I focused my own eyes back upon Mother. She jumped from her leading position, spinning impressively through the air. Then, she plunged her mighty shield into the face of one dwarf, aggressively breaking his nose. Her archaic blade pierced bloodily through another, as she was dancing in her stance. It was as if I was viewing this battle as time itself slowed around me. Mother did not stop there. She continued to fiercely push through these enemies, so effortlessly.

As Mother was now leaving a trail of bodies in her wake, all the shadows that followed Mother burst menacingly from the ground and took their Dragokin forms. Overmortus was the first that I noticed. He hissed as he took physical form and then ripped his vile spear from the darkened Fabrics of nature. Any enemies that were still breathing along Mother's path, Overmortus was soon to forever silence.

Each of these corrupted Shadows were staying near Mother. They formed a defensive circle around her as she continued pushing through, cutting down the dwarves that were foolish enough to charge her with deadly intentions. The Shadows were casting dark and haunting spells, flailing their evilly sharpened weapons, and consuming the Dwarves vilely through the very shadows darkened in the grounds.

My eyes only continued to scan the battlefield. The Ents were steadily positioning themselves next to Mother, secured within the Shadows defense. I noticed Talonux was positioned swiftly within the branches of a nearby tree. One after another he plunged arrows into the hearts of our enemies. There was no end to his volley and every shot ended the intended Dwarves heart near instantly.

Upon closer realization, I noticed a golden aura surrounding his bow and the arrows which were cast from it. With every shot, it was as if I were watching a mystical Dragon hurl fireballs from its mouth. It was such a wonder to witness. Gaining better position, Talonux jumped from one tree to the next, keeping the advantage of higher ground.

As I continued examining the battlefield, I was now realizing that every Warrior bore their own stances. Their styles of fighting varied. From close quarters combat to lethally ranged postures. Still deadly, just in their own menacing ways. My eyes broke sight from Talonux and the other Scouts to continue studying. I had a hunger to understand, a thirst for the knowledge of battle.

Bromyx and Engoryx were too fighting side by side, much like the Shadows and the Scouts were. It seemed every section of the Warriors stayed closely near one another, forming their own individual packs. These monsters of battle, true of Dragokin blood, were swinging their mighty weapons around violently, claiming the lives of our enemies so naturally. From head to toe, hip to hip, they were slicing through the Dwarves, and painting the ground with their blood.

It seemed their weapons shook the ground we fought upon. That their physical powers were truly immense and near impossible to match. I could hear them chuckling as endless waves of lifeless Dwarves were decorating the grounds, that of those foolish enough to engage them. There was no fear to be sought within the hearts of our people, especially not of this pack. It was as if war, battle, was truly what broiled in the veins of our people, our pack.

As the battle continued to wage, we continued furthering our position into the village. Not one Warrior that stood amongst our ranks seemed to be growing tiresome or weakened from this battle. I sensed that this skirmish was already won before it had even started. Though the Dwarves numbers surely outnumbered our own, the skill of battle and prowess did not match between the colliding forces.

The air continued to fill with battle cries, the winds carrying the mixed magical energies and auras, the ground now soaking in the puddles of blood that leaked from our enemies. I was but in the eye of the storm and truly experiencing war, death, and the rage of battle. I could not understand why at this point, the Dwarves did not retreat. We have yet to lose one from our people, yet they have lost more than I could count.

As we were finally within the heart of the village, our Warriors had begun to spread out and clear what remained of our enemies. As the Shadows dispersed, Nemmonis and Overmortus were the only two who remained at Mothers side. There was no sneaking around or being cautious, Mother pushed her trail directly towards those captured and bound in chains, sitting defenselessly in the villages square.

We were not engaging as many foes now. It seemed they had all but exhausted their countless numbers. That what remained of the Dwarven Warriors were now riddled with fear in the presence of our Warriors. Still, sounds of battle filled the air, but not as intensely as when we first started. I felt the atmosphere change a bit, clanging and clashing and cries could still be heard, but it was fewer. Mother and the Shadows seemed to be avoided now. And I felt a sense of relief and pride swell in my chest.

Soon, Vodish and Sorth found their positions nearest Mother too. As our enemy's numbers were dwindling, it seemed this battle would soon be over. Mother was drenched in the blood of our enemies. Her rage was still boiling within her. Nemmonis and Overmortus were too consumed in a haunting rage, blood was even dripping from their mouths like beasts.

"Ents, release those people from the binds that enslave them! Free their spirits of such burden!" Vodish commanded as he slung his now bloodied and ancient spear across his back.

All the Ents broke from Mothers side and were now defensively charging towards the citizens that were rounded up for senseless slaughter. One by one, the Ents crushed all of the chains and their respective locks in their very tightened grips, reducing the metals to mere splinters and dust. The men, women, and children of this Dragokin village were now arming themselves as well, since our enemies still raged through the streets. As soon as the last citizen was released, something happened.

There was a group of Dwarves retreating from the village and the Ents took a hastened notice to this. The leader of the pack speedily grabbed a finely sharpened spear from the back of another. He positioned himself and then cruelly thrusted this ooze covered spear in the retreating Dwarves direction. Surely enough, the spear was on target and burst through the Dwarves body. In that moment, it was as if the Ents lost control of themselves.

Within the blink of an eye, they started charging towards these Dwarves with utmost haste. Dust was kicking up and clouding behind us in the trails. Before we drew too far, I noticed Vodish, and Mother were startled from the actions of the Ents. They too started charging in our direction, and I could only feel this was not of the plan.

Refocusing my attention on what lied ahead, I noticed we were soon on the Dwarves trails. The Ents continued volleying their toxic spears towards them. Then, I noticed familiar arrows with their own golden magical auras zipping hastily from behind us. Each arrow finding their marks in the backs of the retreating dwarves. There was but one Dwarf that remained along the ridgeline. The remaining Ents had him secured tightly against the ground with their vines.

As we approached, the Dwarf stared into my eyes, into my very soul. Blood leaking from his injuries, saliva oozing from his vine covered mouth, he flailed around trying to escape, but the Ents were not releasing him. We held that position as Mother, Vodish, and Talonux were soon to be at our stance. They did not seem impressed at all with the Ents actions. They all seemed furious.

"I should cut you all down and burn your beings!" Mother fumed viciously as she rapidly approached.

"*Quisvale, I apologize for their actions and will take full responsibility* but **calm your rage**," Vodish begged.

Vodish tried placing his hand upon Mother, but she abruptly shook him from doing so. Mother cracked the fabrics of Nydeli and threw her shield and weapon back into the blackened void in which they came from. She was aggressively stomping towards the Ent that I was secured onto. The Ent took notice to this as well and began breaking the vines that secured me.

The fearsome rage within Mother was intensely unbalanced, I could also sense fear and a questioning heartache. As the Ent was struggling to rip his own vines, Mothers sharpened claws pierced viciously into the Ents chest, and with one violent tug she broke me from the Ents being. As Mother began to cradle me within one arm, her other hand begun harnessing extremely powerful magical energies and focusing an intensified bloodlust towards the Ent that appeared to be dying now.

"**QUISVALE!**" Vodish shouted as his own aura brightly emitted from his serious grips, locking tightly onto Mother's shoulders, "**Calm yourself, now!**"

Then, it seemed within that moment, Mother was suddenly broken free from the rage that consumed her. Vodish's own aura was now consuming both Mother and me. Our surroundings, warm, flooding our bodies with a soothing calmness. Mother was still hesitant, though her rage was finally dispersing. Mother looked down to me and I noticed a blackened tear rolling down her cheek.

As Vodish released his grips from Mother, she was soon to tremble onto her weakening knees. Mother just pulled me against her face and if not within such close quarters, you would not have heard her whimper and weep. I just wrapped my arms around Mother's neck and began to snuggle against her. As Mother was finding her dignity again, Vodish walked over to the Ent that seemed to be dying.

Vodish's hand had not stopped glowing, and he placed it upon the open chest of his dying companion, his aura consuming the Ent and calming its spirit. The Ent stopped twitching from the intense pain it was suffering, and Vodish's aura continued to surround its entire body. The Ent just placed his hand upon Vodish's and relaxed the very soul that was pulsating within.

Vodish's tone sincerely chanted, *"Halg's Mausoleum"*, underneath his sorrow filled breath. Slowly, he gracefully pressed the Ent back into Nydeli's surface. The Ent began breaking down, vines releasing from one another, and the creature was shedding to crumbles. It shrunk to a single vine and slithered back into the dirt.

The tension within the air was thick, even I could sense there would be confrontational questions to follow. There was no heartache or hate coming from Vodish, as if he wanted to struggle to understand Mother's actions. The remaining Ents just kneeled before Vodish as he began pacing towards Mother. I could feel Vodish was soon to speak but was unexpectedly interrupted.

Over the ridgeline we could hear thunderous trampling sounds, the faint voices soon to be recognized as their own war cries, Talonux was soon to approach the ridge, "**M'LADY, RETREAT!**" he shouted as he gathered a handful of arrows from his quiver.

The moment Talonux ordered for retreat, an opposing volley of artillery had begun to cast an overwhelming shadow over our position. As we all looked up, it was in that moment I felt devastation within the hearts of those in the village. Everyone had begun to disorderly scatter, searching for immediate shelter from this horizon stretched bombardment. The Warriors of our pack were charging directly towards our position with their hands and arms above their heads, mystical shields luminating above those absent of heavily fortified and physical shields.

Talonux still stood upon the ridgeline of incoming battle, violently launching handfuls of arrows as the remaining Warriors rallied on his position. The looks upon their faces turned from glorious smiles of a won battle to dreary frowns of misfortune. They all began readying their defensive stances and vicious weapons. Mother was soon to find her own ground and positioned herself nearest the ridge. Vodish now protectively postured next to us, just focusing his intensive awareness on Mother. That is when I could feel a sudden intense change within Mother's heart.

"*Vodish.*" Mother whispered as one of her eyes darkened and the other shined brightly.

Without word, Vodish took me from Mothers warm embrace. This time, he did not wrap me within vines, but merely slung me over his shoulder as he closely followed Mother. She was slowly pacing towards the ridgeline as she had begun harnessing an overpowering amount of energy. Mother's claws widened, palms facing Nydeli's surface. It seemed she was absorbing streams of reddened lightning, divine powers from the highly energetic core of Nydeli herself.

These lashing streams of magical energies entering Mother were wild. The auras they were emitting were not that of Mother's but mixed with varying shades. Reddened and gold sparks were flickering within the waves of iridescent rays, their illuminations dancing and intertwining with her own. The Warriors in our presence cautiously stepped from Mother's path, startled as they too were witnessing such an indifferent surge of overwhelming power. Mother's wings spread wide as she casted a mighty shadow down the ridgeline.

Vodish followed closely to Mother, we were soon to recognize why Talonux, and the others had fiercely racing hearts. Another massive wave of our enemies was aggressively storming towards the village. We thought this battle was over, that this village was now free and liberated of our enemies. We soon discovered otherwise.

Our enemy's numbers were now tenfold what we had already faced. Talonux continued to exhaustingly volley his own arrows directly into their oncoming path. I watched as he was slaying many Dwarves at a time. Mother was soon to place her hand upon Talonux's shoulder.

"*M'Lady....*" Talonux trembled as Mother began taking up her own posture.

Mother's voice in this moment seemed different, as if it were echoing within itself, speaking down an empty hallway, *"Without darkness, there is no light. Without chaos, there is no peace. Father lend me your forsaken strength, Mother, give me your protective wings.* **DRAXPERILS PROTECTION AND TALONTUINS WINGS!"** Mother shouted as one hand pushed from the ridgeline and the other reached towards the skies.

    The burst of magical energies that exploded from Mother's being was potently magnificent. The power alone pushed many of the Warriors off their own balance and shaking them from their stances. Vodish was the only one to stand vigilant as such a force whipped around us. The magical streams that were emitting from Mother's palms were viciously tearing through the rock hardened grounds. One burst of energy bearing the purest of white streams, the other darkened with varying shades of purple.

    As I followed the brightened stream zipping through towards the skies, the image of a magnificent Dragon illuminated high above. Just before the enemy's artillery could find their targets on our position, this spell Mother had casted begun reducing the impending threat of deadly weaponry to mere ashes. The images of the dragons that shined so brightly above were flying magnificently over our position, shielding us from everything our enemies launched towards us.

Then, I looked towards the darkened stream that Mother cast down the ridgeline. As these haunting energies were soaking into Nydeli's surface I could vaguely see what was truly happening. There were silhouettes of beings pulling defensive barriers from the portals of another realm, charging head on with our incoming enemies. For as far as my eyes could see, these darkened mirages of a summoned army conjured hastily.

Mother soon erupted with pain as these energies began to slowly disperse from her body. I could feel she barely had the strength to muster her own words as she hit her knees, "*We have been bought little time,* **Gather all those inside the village and retreat towards our masses**! *If the defenses hold, we shall be concealed within the shadows before our enemies find us.*"

"**M'Lady**!" the Warriors worryingly replied while shakenly saluting Mother. Shortly afterwards, the Warriors pushed towards the village, shouting for the desperate retreat, and proceeded to follow Mother's orders.

"***Vodish**, I have opened my Father's portal and his forces may only be able to buy you enough time to find concealment within the shadows. Tell Charmortus that my love is everlasting, and that he must seek a true future for our child.* **I will keep the portals open so long as I breathe**." Mother pleaded as her aura, her very light, began flickering brilliantly.

"*Quisvale*. Though your actions are hasty, I am still proud of how far you have come." Vodish replied as he kneeled next to Mother and secured me within her arms, "Though the forsaken blood runs through your veins, you have shown your people that innocent lives should not be forfeited. Even at the possible cost of your own life."

As Mother struggled to get back onto her feet, she whispered through her broken tone, "*I fear there is not enough time currently bought for a successful retreat. **Please**, **Vodish**, take my child with you and do not turn back. If... If I can only hold these spells and keep their portals open...*"

Mother's heart was beginning to break from the solid force in which I have succumbed to my entire life. Her very essence of life was beyond intoxicating and now, now it was riddled with fear. I clenched onto Mother tightly as her eyes began to drizzle. Then, Vodish's strengthened grasp grabbed hold of Mother and helped her to her feet.

"*Now now*, **child**. Never forget the trials that formed you into the Dragokin, the Shield Maiden that you are, and to ask a mentor to forsake his pupil, **that is ludicrous**. Come, lead these masses towards a trail of safety. Towards a trail with a destined future," Vodish replied while forcibly lifting Mother and I onto Sorth's saddle.

"*Vodish, NO!*" Mother cried out just before vines secured us tightly onto Sorth and she hesitated against their strengthening bind.

"**Sorth**, *my girl*, lead them far from here. Lead them to their destination and then find yourself free at last. Our time together has been honored with your presence alone." Vodish pleaded as he placed his forehead against Sorths, "Halg will finally return my essence to which the gardens they grew!"

Sorth screeched subtly, nudging her nose against his chest. Her own tears drizzling down her emerald scales. Mother continued to weep as well, joining Sorth in this heartbreaking moment. Mother never ceased from trying to break free of the vines that entangled us. Crying out for Vodish as he turned his back from us and paced towards the ridgeline. I did not share the same heartache both Mother and Sorth were experiencing. I could feel though the newly found glory rising from Vodish. There was now an endless fire burning within him, such a flame could spark the torches wielded by a million men.

The elderly Orc had begun stripping the armor from his body as he met the ridge. Deepened scars and blemishes of suffering covered his moss-colored body. He but dawned only an anciently embedded cloth around his hips and golden talon-like boots still strapped to his feet. As he began spinning his ancient spear around, now illuminating brightly, a vast amount of magical energies were pulling directly into his presence. This power, beyond what Mother had just dispersed, choked those close enough to be embodied within the presence of such dense energies.

Sorth screeched one last time before turning from our location, Mothers own cries matched that of the rapidly retreating Raptors. As Sorth strode forward, furthering our position from Vodish, both Mother and I could not turn our eyes from him. The ridgeline was soon to be consumed with his impeccable green aura. Hundreds of Ents began rising from Nydeli, readily armed, and anxiously shaking for orders. Vodish looked back towards us one last time, his unmistaken glance staring through our souls, then he burst with even more immense power.

"HALG'S FURY!" Vodish cried out while gusts of winds violently lashed and swirled along the ridgeline, his risen army began to charge.

Just before Vodish and his army of nature dispersed completely from our eyesight, we witnessed the mass collision between the opposing forces and Vodish's summoned lines of formidable defenses. The battle cries grew louder, and the melody of battle was soon to echo through the winds again. We gained more distance from Vodish, the sights of an empty village relieving to our eyes, and our retreating forces trails were now scurrying up the mountain.

Mother just gripped onto me tightly as her heart continued to tremble. At first, we thought this to be a battle without loss, but now Mother displayed that an unforgiving sacrifice has just been made. Sorth's heart matched that of Mother's, but she continued to push up the mountain.

As we were nearing the top of the mountain, Nemmonis and Overmortus were awaiting our caravan. If not for carefully watching, I would not have noticed the thin fabric between our world and that of the cloaked dimensions the shadows were leading us. One by one our retreating numbers continued the trail that followed the remaining of our masses.

Sorth stopped just before the threshold to enter the concealment of the shadows. She slowly turned her head, snapping the tightened vines between her sharpened teeth, our release now easily attempted. Sorth crouched towards a flattened stone so that Mother could effortlessly dismount her. As Mother exhaustingly slid us from atop the mount, Sorth's worrying eyes looked down toward the village, whimpering as she truly feared what was to come.

The tethered aura that luminated between Vodish and Sorth had began flickering. Sorth snappishly took notice to this as well. Mother was soon to realize the shattering cracks that were looming within the tether as well. Mother grabbed hold of Sorth with tears still rolling heavily down her cheeks. Attempting to calm the now racketing mind of the ferocious beast.

"Sorth, come. Please." Mother begged as Sorth was twitching with devastation pouring from her heart.

Then, the tether that was suddenly shattering, flashing cracked beams of light, was soon to completely disseminate and vanish with the winds. Sorth screeched loudly and her desperate cry shattered our ears. There was now a deepened heartache vehemently emitting from Sorth. She glanced over to Mother and pushed us towards the trail with her nose. Mother gripped onto her tightly, attempting to pull her with us. But we could sense her heart was already fated with decision. She fiercely broke from Mothers grips and burst with hostility in the direction of the village.

"*NO!*" Mother shouted as she attempted to grab hold of Sorth by any means.

Nemmonis and Overmortus were quick with restraining Mother's rash actions. As Mother ferociously fought against their grips, I could feel her intense magical energies pulsing abruptly. Her own aura emitting eyes began to flash and dampen as well. Mother continued to cry, and her strength was severely weakening. We were slowly vanishing within the shadows, now evading discovery from any sight set from the crumbling village.

"**M'Lady Quisvale**, *what is done*, **is done**," Overmortus concerned as Nemmonis was now casting a wicked spell, painting ancient symbols within thin air, sealing the very essence of such a mystic concealment that gloomed around us. Shadows cast around us, there was a new silence, a silence that would forever echo the essence of undeniable pain, of complete loss, of true heartache.

CHAPTER SEVEN
WITHIN THE DREAM REALM, THERE IS A VOICE

Since that fateful day, the day we lost Vodish and Sorth, thoughts of veering from the concealed path no longer crossed Mother's mind. Such a devastating event took its time to finally settle within her heart and mind. Her soul suffered dearly upon that day, and I knew it would take divinity itself to heal such wounds inflicted upon her. I knew this because she did not stand as strong or proud for many suns to come.

The trail thus far was covered in the blood and ashes of fellow countrymen and women, children, and animals. Villages were reduced to charcoaled rubble. The air reeked of death and smoke. The enemy that hunted us had no mercy for those who frolicked in the fields and mountains of Bundok ng Dragon. The Land of Dragons, the throne atop Nydeli, forged from the very breath of Dragons themselves.

Mother and Father would always tell stories of this home, our home. They preached about the sacred grounds and memorial sites. Buried within these lands not only Dragons, but also the late War Chiefs and Shield Maidens. Heroic symbols that faithfully ruled these lands for centuries. That no matter how far a Dragon flies, Bundok ng Dragon would always be the beacon of light that would lead them home.

There were not many memories of this home that I could recall. I had been sheltered within the security of our house for as long as I could remember. There was still much more growing for the libraries within my mind, so my thoughts were still clouded. There was not much stored within my psyche to even process life entirely, yet enough to understand when our journey truly began.

Before we were forced to lead this retreat, what I do remember was Mother always stayed home with me. Father would leave at the sight of days new light. There were not many times we would leave our home, and the times we did we would not stray too far from it. Our home was concealed within the density of forestry. It was as if Mother bore fear for something, or someone. Yet she did not display such, her actions and sheltering would convince one otherwise.

Even now seeing the world in such despair, even as tragedy unfolded within these lands, my eyes were still amazed to witness what truly was beyond the walls of our house. Rough and wavy mountains that overlapped from horizon to horizon. The rocky ridgelines resembling that of a Dragons spine. Vibrant green fields that spread at the feet of these monstrous mountains, crystal blue rivers slithering through the deepened crimson caverns of these lands.

As our retreat continued, my eyes finally broke from such wonderous scenery. I was detailing everything outlined within the days sinking light. The thunderous clatter of footsteps and rattling of steel plates chimed within our ears. Our eyes bore witness to Father and the remaining forces finally arriving to our forward leading position.

Though longer apart than anyone expected, our people would finally be whole again. I remember it clearly as we were resting within ruby rock caverns. Rapid diamond tides whipped viciously below while hastily flowing towards the distant horizon.

Mother expressed the purest of rejoice when Father was sighted at the lead of this incoming pack. She gripped onto me, and we rushed towards Father joyously. Just as Mother expressed such delight, others were soon to join her as well only upon sighting their loved one's return. A collective breath of relief was had, and a feeling of warmth and love floated in the space between us. Once there was lost hope and despair, now the hearts and souls of those around had been fully restored.

"**My dearest!**" Father shouted towards us.

"***Charmortus!***" Mother cried out.

There was a long and warm embrace between Mother and Father when the two collided. I could feel their hearts fluttering as I was crunched between the two. Father broke his grip before Mother and grabbed both of our faces by the chin. Fresh wounds of battle marked Father's face and chest, but such injuries did not falter his thoughts. It felt like it had been so long, perhaps that is why we all lingered a hair longer when we took in each other's gazes, trying to take in what the other had seen.

"*There is much we need to...*" Mother whispered before Father placed his finger upon her soft trembling lips.

"There is nothing in this world that needs to happen other than embracing this moment, **Quisvale**," Father replied as he pulled us back into his arms, "The Shadows sent word of the trail thus far, *you need not explain*. To see the love of my life, and my child that sparks even greater flame than I, is all that I need to bear witness to."

Mother's smile stretched ear to ear and her eyes began pooling with warmed tears. She clenched onto Father tighter, and I did as well. There was much bliss to be found within all those around, yet this journey we embarked was nowhere near its end. Within such devastating times, the times of magic and folklore, it was best to find peace whenever and wherever it could be discovered.

Good thing it was that we took a moment to be released from the crisis ever evolving around us, because we were soon to be approached by a Warrior of our pack,

"My Chief, the Commanders await your words."

Father broke from Mother with a soft and subtle kiss, "Yes Aurumscale, rally the Commanders and order our men to aid those in need. We shall discuss furthering our distance."

"My Chief," Aurumscale acknowledged before bowing and dashing into the crowds.

"Quisvale, see to it our people are ready for this continued trail. It will take but a year without obstacles to reach the coast. We shall see the end of this journey and provide our people with safe passage to the rest of their lives," Father sternly addressed before dispersing into the crowds as well.

As Mother was pacing through the resting masses, I remained latched onto her shoulders, bouncing, and bobbing around. Witnessing as the people once displayed fear in their eyes for Mother, now the purest of love towards her emitted from their hearts.

Mother did not skip a beat, she began ordering Warriors to aid, ensuring others had plenty of water, and ordering Warriors to assist those in need. Medicus began dispersing and tending to the injured, food and water were spread amongst all. Even through what we had endured, I felt there would still be a long journey ahead.

The sun stretched across the skies, and the moon was breaking the distant horizon before Father returned to us. The look upon his face was serious. Yet, hope pumped from his heart whilst enlightening those around. As Father grabbed hold of Mothers hand, he led us towards the lead of the newly massed formation.

Once at the lead, Shadows began dispersing into their blackened mists and pushing towards the dawning horizon. Warriors had begun spreading out and guarding our caravan from every angle. The Commanders followed closely behind Father, and we were now setting foot onto the journey towards the sun.

Through this journey I was in and out of consciousness more than usual. When I was awake, we were either resting or walking. There were no battles, or obstacles to be met to keep my mind from slumber. Within Mother's and Father's arms, I found utmost comfort. There was a sense of safety in their presence that induced the dream realm.

When in Father's arms, or balanced upon his broad shoulders, he would point out different Warriors amongst our ranks. All decorated ceremoniously in their own different appearances. Continuously explaining his reasons for believing that I too would find the strength to become such. He would place me onto the grounds standing on my own two feet, forcing me to attempt walking with my own two legs. The weight of my wings would always throw me off balance and drive me to meet the harsh and hardened grounds.

I found myself to be in Mother's arms quickly after injuring myself. Father's efforts never ceased in his attempts to get me to walk. She would snap and bicker towards Father as he would just burst into laughter and praise. When I was in Mother's arms, she would focus my eyes onto the beautiful scenery surrounding us through our lands. Pointing out the littlest details that surely made such images whole.

Beyond the lessons Mother and Father preached along our journey, there was not much for my mind to truly digest. That of the highest remembrance were the ashes spread across the lands. The villages reduced to ruins, and the bodies of those who possessed no magical energies were left to rot underneath the days brilliant light. Under our circumstances there was no time for proper burial or ceremony for those that were lost. We had only hoped Talontuin, the Dragon Goddess of Life, had found those lost souls and guided them underneath her wings.

This day was halfway aged. The sun had stretched across the marvelous skies and was soon bound to meet the dawning horizon. We were finally on the coast of Bundok ng Dragon, where these sacred lands met the ocean. There was not much vegetation nearby, only hardened rockface and fallen defenses from the recent breach.

As we approached the coast of Bundok ng Dragon, my Father, Charmortus Gray-Flame, the Chief to these lands, the gentle lover to my Mother, the War Chief written in history, had dispersed of what forces were left among us,

"TWIN BLADES AND TOWER SHIELDS, CREATE AN IMMEASURABLE AND UNBREAKABLE DEFENSE AROUND THIS POSITION!" Father had ordered.

The Twin Blades and Tower Shields were the fiercest of Warriors throughout all the lands, Dragokin that wielded primitive, yet savage blades in their hands from the moment of birth. All they have ever known and trained for was battle. Most lacked in natural magical abilities, but they made up for that in brute strength and strategic battle knowledge.

All these Warriors were decorated in magical obsidian armor and a variety of weapons. Typically, the Twin Blades mastered their abilities dual wielding weapons, whereas the Tower Shields focused on wielding two handed weaponry. Every Warrior from both sections of our Dragokin army were forces not to be reckoned with.

"YES CHIEF!" the soldiers shouted as they saluted Father, and shortly afterward began to muster upon their positions.

"HIDDEN SHADOWS AND FORWARD SCOUTS, PUSH BEYOND THOSE DEFENSES AND ALLOW YOUR EYES AND EARS TO BE OUR FIRST LINE OF DEFENSE!" Father ordered to the second section of the fighting force.

The Hidden Shadows and Forward Scouts were much different than the Twin Blades and Tower Shields. These Warriors did not focus on frontline battle. They would first be positioned beyond the line of defense, then as the enemies approached, they would activate their traps and rally behind the frontline.

The Hidden Shadows did not consist of many Warriors among them. Only a handful, but of the deadliest intentions. These Warriors possessed magnificent magical abilities and were the quickest on the battlefields. Their obsession with dark magic consumed most of their minds, but their loyalty was bound to Dragokin banners.

Scouts. All Scouts were generally the same. They would just be positioned differently throughout the battlefield. These Warriors were more focused on ranged tactics and covering the battlefields with sheets of arrows. When their hands were forced to engage in close quarters combat, they were equipped with deadly daggers or short blades. Also, their physical abilities allowed them to dance through the battlefield as their blades painted death upon those within their path.

"**YES CHIEF!**" shouted the Hidden Shadows and Scouts as they too saluted Father and took their positions.

As the sound of marching echoed throughout the coast, Father stood there stoically as the fighting forces found their positions. All that remained now were the families of these lands, the Scholars and their Apprentice Casters, and the Royal Guard to the Heart of Bundok ng Dragon.

"**Royal Guards**, *as you always do*, **you may light your own path and find that the Heart of Bundok ng Dragon be secured**. Whether your plans are to continue with us towards the Twelve Kingdoms, or rally elsewhere, the choice is in your Commanders hands." Father preached to the nearby Warriors.

The Royal Guards did not bolster many in their forces, but these Warriors had been offered anything their heart's desired to protect Royalty from other lands. Their loyalty would forever be with Bundok ng Dragon. Such a loyalty had never been bought or bribed.

There was a handful of them protecting a heavily secured crate. There was nothing special about this crate, other than the fact that it took eight Warriors to carry the massive chest, and that it seemed to be constricted with magical chains. The chest itself looked to be ancient.

"**Charmortus, my Brother at Arms,** you have given the Heart of Bundok ng Dragon safe passage to the coast, and now it is our journey to secure it and plan for what the future holds for our lands. We shall rally once again my friend, once all is secure!" a strange man decorated in golden armor had explained to Father.

"The Heart must always be secure, Brother, but that does not mean you must break path now." Father replied.

"You know the Heart does not belong in the Twelve Kingdoms. Hengtuin will surely continue to light our path and show us the way. He has brought us this far, but his fire does not merge our paths any further," The strange man said before saluting Father and shaking his hand.

This man seemed so strange to me, as well as the Royal Guards, because their faces were unknown. Covered in a golden dragon skull helm, their wings were even disguised underneath gold-plated armor. No one truly knew who the Protectors of the Heart were. Only that their Oath was taken within the depths of Nydeli, and forever to be sworn to protect the Heart of Bundok ng Dragon.

Father returned a salute to this man and shook his hand firmly. He pulled the man close and whispered something in his ear. As they released their grips, the man chuckled and patted Father's shoulder. Soon after, the strange man ordered for the Royal Guards to take flight and soar beyond the horizon.

As the Royal Guards were positioning themselves along the coastline, they had begun securing the chest to heavy rings on their armor. There was but one Royal Guard that pulled my interest, because this individual was looking directly into my soul. The remaining guards continued to ready themselves, whereas this one just continued glaring at me.

Just before the Royal Guards were ordered to leap from the cliff, it seemed the eyes of this Royal Guard had flickered a hundred colors in a mere instant, yet I was the only one to notice this. As the eye holes in their helm returned to a blackened concealment, this Royal Guard, I could hear her faint chuckle, and then off they were into the great distance above the open seas.

Once all the politics of Father's position were settled, he began to walk towards me and Mother. His marvelous armor clanking together and shimmering in what little sunlight remained. There was a stern look upon Father's face until his eyes met Mother's, then a smile broke through the shell of his seriousness.

Mother was holding me in her arms. We were silently sitting oceanside on a cliff. Father stood beside her; gold trimmed obsidian armor decorating his body. Our entire pack of Dragokin were behind us making camp. Hundreds of Dragokin were waiting for the encouraging words Father would preach.

Father turned from us and faced the masses of our clan. As he paced towards the crowds, he unsheathed his blades and glanced from the Eastern horizon to the Western. Smoke waved in the distance of our homeland. It was as if our broken lands were sending us off, with one last farewell.

"Our lands may have been lost, but not forever! The prophecy speaks of three dragons returning and claiming that in which we have lost! Restoring the order which chaos destroyed! **Hengtuin has set us on our path, and now, more so than ever, we must faithfully follow!"** Father shouted as he raised his swords with pride.

I could feel the spirits of those surrounding us become lifted with Fathers words alone. A wave of weapons and hands filled the air. The roaring of hundreds was consuming the skies fearsomely. Such a roar shook the very ground beneath us, sending a chill down my spine.

"**Prepare a hasty camp for the night my brothers and sisters, sons and daughters**. For this might be the last of nights that we are allowed to enjoy with those whom we surround ourselves. By first light of the new day, we will soar through the skies towards the Twelve Kingdoms. The Great Seas are vast, and can be treacherous, even in the skies," Father ended, before our pack continued to burrow in and make camp.

I have only heard tales of the Twelve Kingdoms. A place where all races from all walks of life live amongst one another. Where no one towers over the other and everyone is kin. Where all lives are protected underneath all the heavens. Father promised that the lives of our kin would no longer be at risk in such a place.

Father returned to me and Mother near the oceanside cliff. He placed his hands upon Mother's shoulders and gave an ever so gentle kiss on her neck. The sun was setting off in the distance before us, filling the sky with magnificent crimson shades. A cool breeze brushed over us from the ocean's subtle tides.

"***What is it my love****? What is this that I sense within your heart?*" Father asked as he sat down next to us.

"Everything we have been through, everything we have lost. All of this upon our sacred grounds. It does not make sense to me. Draxux has never been so easily breached," Mother replied with a most concerned tone.

"There are questions in this world that may never be answered, my love. All we can do is continue fighting the good fight and ensure the prophecy is fulfilled. Hengtuin has lit our path with his very flames, so we must follow. Draxux will not be under siege forever, **I swear that with my very breath**!" Father vowed while gripping Mother's hand.

"Your strength alone could move this world, that strength now lives within our beautiful son," Mother replied as she kissed Father's hand and looked deeply into my eyes.

"Yes, and it is that strength that will someday surpass even Hengtuin himself!" Father cheered!

As Father made that bold statement, the masses of our clan began to beat their fists against their chests while chanting, **"DRAGO!"**

"And with that strength, Hengtuin will light the righteous path for our kin, that path being rightfully centered here! BUNDOK NG DRAGON!" Father continued to claim.

"DRAGO!" the masses continued to chant.

Mother handed me over to Father. He gripped me firmly and held me high while resting his head within Mother's lap. The scars of war marked his face, neck, and arms. Eyes deeply reddened with a gray haze through them. He displayed no signs of pain or weakness, as if those very scars were reminders of his strength and survival.

Father placed me on his chest and wrapped his arms around me. Even War Chiefs have hearts that can beat gently, especially for those of their own blood. Although seen as heartless and emotionless creatures, War Chiefs are still simple beings. They are nothing more than what we were all made of, apart from their unmatchable strength and war-torn minds.

Mother draped her wings around us as we all found comfort in one another's company. We laid there for a moment. In the silence of our own solitude. Peace. That is what we found as we fell into a slumber. Though war torn, that night we found the last bit of comfort together under the heavens and within our homeland.

The sun had begun to set. The sounds of making camp were finding a halt. Every Dragokin in our pack were beginning to lay to rest as well. Only the sound of a subtle breeze soon whispered over our massive camp. Not one soul knew this would only be the lull before the storm.

*"**DRAGO**" was being chanted as I sat there in a dark room. The whispering winds echoed within this chamber as my eyes began to adjust to the darkness. I was not me, or at least the present me. I seemed to be older than I truly was.*

*There was nobody else in this room with me. It was cold, had me shivering to my bones. "**DRAGO!**" continued to echo within my mind, within this room. Then, one by one, candles began to light themselves. As these candles began to fill the area, I was noticing ancient carvings upon the walls.*

*I struggled to get up, as if my body were bound to this position by chains. As if the weight of the world were upon me. "**DRAGO!**" and this chant started to settle, to become noiseless. At the end of this room was a massive steel gate. The candlelight revealed magical chains around this gate.*

I glanced for a moment before these deeply black and reddened eyes opened beyond the gate's threshold. There was a fire within these eyes. Like wild flames waving in fierce winds. It was at that moment that there was a deep, growling voice.

"Ikaw si Drago! Ikaw ang Propesiya! Maging ang Dragon na iyong ipinanganak na maging!"

As these words were spoken, smoke began to emit from beyond the gate. The very bars were engulfed in ashy gray flames. The smoke began to cover the floor, consuming the once lit candles, now dousing them out. The room was beginning to slowly fade to darkness once again.

I tried to speak, but it was as if my very words were stripped from my mind and my mouth sewn shut. There was this pain in my ears after the dark, mysterious voice had spoken. This tongue that was spoken echoed through my head. This art of words I knew, it was of the ancient Draconic language. A language that has been long forgotten within the world.

The room had been fully consumed in this smoke, my eyes and chest now enduring the fiery pain which was being inflicted upon me. I began to suffocate and struggle to keep my eyes open. The voice had now shouted through the darkness,

"GISING NA!"
"GO, NOW!"

This dream, it had shaken me from my slumber. I was soon to realize that it was just that, a dream. That my reality still stood. Father and Mother were still sleeping soundlessly while I was tucked between their loving embraces. Snuggled between the safety of their very beings.

As I began to snuggle against Mother's warm body, that is when everything came crashing down on us like a fierce tidal wave. Draconic war horns sounded in the distance. Echoing throughout the lands and penetrating our ears. One by one they sounded off loudly waking the entire camp just before the days new light.

Mother was quick to shelter me within her arms. Father even quicker to arming himself. Both Mother and Father stood vigilantly as the horns continued to sound off. The look within their eyes was worrisome. As if they have never heard war horns sound off before.

"***Those horns, those are not....***" Mother quickly snapped. "**Yes**, *my love*, **they are**," Father responded before Mother could finish, "**Draxxux has fallen!**"

CHAPTER EIGHT
ANCIENT MAGIC

The horns continued to echo, becoming louder and louder. These horns, though, were not like the ones I had heard before. They were much deeper in tone, and they continued to stretch throughout the lands. The horns that the fighting forces were equipped with yielded a higher pitch, and occasionally broke between calls.

*"Those are coming from the **Citadel**; **it cannot be true!**"* Mother snapped at Father.

"Those horns have not sounded in centuries, and the Dragokin in charge of sounding them know the severity of their call. The Citadel has fallen my love. Along with it, any lasting hope for the survival of those around," Father desperately admitted.

Soon after, the familiar sound of the fighting force's war horns had begun sounding off. This sound was even quicker to pull Father's attention. This brought news that the enemies were near, that our retreat must push forward with the utmost swiftness.

Two Dragokin Scouts decorated lightly with leather and beast pelts, armed with mystical bows, came rushing towards us. Even from the distance I could witness the worrisome looks upon their faces, that they did not come bearing good news.

They were descending from the skies with extreme rapidity, the look of exhaustion pasted upon their faces. As they neared, details of battle were inflicted upon them. They landed before Father, almost breathless.

"War Chief, a vast army approaches from the North. They ambushed the Shadows and took with them captures from the Scouting fleets! They hit us hard before we could become aware of their presence!" one of the Scouts mustered through his lost breath.

"This cannot be true, Scout! HOW?!" Father said with rage.

While finding his own breath, the other Scout replied, *"This happened before our eyes could adjust,* **War Chief.** *They were silent through the night, and even our best could not have detected them.* **We have gravely failed....**"

"We were only able to retreat in small forces; we have signaled the defensive line to take posture. Your orders are our commands, what will be our next move, **War Chief**?" the first Scout continued as they kneeled before Father.

"**Find your ground Scouts and continue the rally on this ridge**! Signal the remaining Scouting masses on the defenseless and I shall take the Warriors North. Once the rally is complete you will follow the orders of your Shield Maiden! How long until engagement with our foes?" Father responded while pulling the Scouts to their feet.

"I give them until the days new light to be at our defensive posture, War Chief." The other Scout responded.

"Then before the sun breaks the horizon, we will give the innocent time to take flight and maneuver out of artilleries reach!" Father ordered, "My love, set our kin on the right path and may the winds guide us swiftly to the Twelve Kingdoms. Remember to follow the Southern horizon and we shall be with you shortly!" Father asked of Mother.

"Yes, my love. Know that I expect you by my side no later than the sun's last light!" Mother said as she embraced him within her warm and nurturing arms.

While between them in their gracious embrace, I could feel their hearts fluttering, that within one another's presence, there was an unbreakable love. Even in the face of danger, their affection endured. No time was needed to express such love, yet it felt it ever lasted and was timeless of its own.

Mother released her nurturing grip and turned towards the gathering masses. She ordered those close enough to begin taking flight course towards the Southern horizon, and that the nearby Scouts begin lighting a path for those to follow. She also ordered them to take only what was necessary for the flight over the open oceans.

By the masses, Dragokin were abandoning our steadfast camp. Leaving behind what they could, and only taking what little they needed. Each Dragokin was fearlessly leaping from the edge of the cliff and spreading their wings wide. There was a subtle breeze that swept around us, just enough to assist in our retreat through the skies.

"Forward fighting position, rally with the defensive line! Forward Scouts, lead the innocent South, drop your position below theirs in a defensive flight maneuver! Flank Scouts take your positions to the East and the West! Let us give these bastards what they came for!" Father shouted, and the Warriors of our pack began to swiftly follow Father's orders.

So fluent and organized, the brute Warriors dashed towards their positions as ordered. I could sense no hesitation within their hearts. Dragokin are prideful beings. War, being that which we take most pride in. Father soon took flight and dashed towards the rear of the masses retreating, directly to the front lines of war.

Mother held me firmly within her arms, patiently waiting for all the others to clear the cliff. She was not only the bride to our War Chief, but also the Shield Maiden of our clan. Counted amongst the strongest and most fearsome Shield Maidens in all the lands. With Father's and Mother's strength together, our clan had much faith within their leadership, that much I could sense within their hearts.

Over the Northern Ridge I witnessed faint figures storming over the hills in inequitable numbers. Artillery began to shower over the defensive posture like a heavy rain. The clashing of steel and war cries filled the air in the distance. I could sense slight worry in Mother's heart, that what we witnessed before our own eyes, was more than they had ever faced before.

Mother was soon to find a nearby Scout. Dragokin Scouts were not decorated like the Dragokin Warriors. Their armor was light; either bound by leather, or beast pelts, some feathered in branches and leaves to provide a greater disguise. Quick on their feet but lacked in strength compared to those of the Warriors.

Each battle born Dragokin was easily recognizable by how they decorated themselves. It was the order and structure that we Dragokin abode by, formalities of the past. Heavy obsidian armor for Warriors, light but durable armor for Scouts, and cloths forged with Hengtuin's flames for scholars of battle.

"**You, Scout**, what is your name?" Mother ordered to a nearby Dragokin Scout.

The Scout Mother had pointed out was quick to realize whom beckoned the order. Without word to the others nearby, he advanced towards Mother with a certain pride in his step. Upon landing in front of her, he kneeled with the traditional salute. As he was preparing his words, he unveiled his hood and answered,

"**I am Draxfur of the Mountains M'Lady!**"

"**Find your ground young one, now is not the time for customs**!" Mother ordered over the bellowing of our retreat, "**Once the last of the innocent have descended, I will need you next to me while I signal for the retreat!**"

"**Your words are my command M'Lady!**" Draxfur responded with a steady tone.

We stood by the cliff while the masses of our clan were making haste off the edge. There was no order, no structure. Just the panic of retreat and the hope to stay alive. Some of the elderly would fall amongst the chaos and Mother was right there to get them back upon their feet. This Scout, Draxfur, faithfully followed closely to assist Mother with the retreating forces.

As the last Dragokin descended off the cliff, Mother handed me over to Draxfur. He looked frightened at the sight of a young Dragoling like me. He was holding me awkwardly as Mother smiled and asked, "*Your first time holding a young one?*"

"**Yes M'Lady! I do not wish to harm your child with clumsiness.**" Draxfur stated as he continued to position me awkwardly in his arms.

Mother adjusted his hands so that he held a firm grip on me. I could sense that the moment Mother placed her hands on his own, his entire being became calm. The nervous feeling within his heart vanished, and his blood even flowed slower. I noticed that there was a subtle aura of silver dancing and swirling around Mother's hands.

"*Grip him firmly and leave your worries behind young Scout. This is but the easiest of tasks you could ever be called upon,*" Mother whispered while gazing deeply within his eyes.

"*Yes M'Lady!*" Draxfur responded with an audible exhale, a new sense of calm washing over him.

Soon after, Mother turned to the Northern ridge and her body became consumed in an immaculate gray aura. Her wings spread wide, and she took up a defensive support posture. Bright gray emblems glowed on her wings and began shifting towards her hands.

"Young Draxfur, what do you know of the relationship between battle and magic?" Mother asked, as we could feel her energies rising.

"Well, I am a Scout M'Lady. My arrows are guided by Hengtuin, and his very flames light their path," Draxfur responded.

"This may prove true young one, but there is a deeper meaning to magic and the bond it shares with every battle. For centuries, magic has been used within wars as weapons, but most have forgotten that the strongest of magic is that of defense, *to protect those whom the caster wishes,*" Mother said as we continued to witness magical energies seep from Nydeli's surface and circulate around her. "Also, it is not just about casting the magic, chanting the spells, or projecting the energies. *Timing, patience, and knowledge speak volumes over hasty actions!*"

I gave a little smile at my Mothers insistence of giving a small lesson to a Scout, even in the midst of all that unfolded around us. Underneath Mother's breath, I could vaguely hear the chant of an ancient language, the Dragon's Tongue. The air began to whirl around us, the wind itself becoming a gray illumination, and pebbles from the cliff began to rise. Once all the ancient emblems covered her arms she shouted, **"HENGTUINS PROTECTION!"**

As a massive stream of light burst from Mother's hands into the heavens, it seemed as if dragons themselves were dancing within the clouds. The clouds above had split and revealed a most interesting sight; a sky the color of silver, with a glow behind it that casted a moon-like hue that lit up the faces of those below.

Shortly afterwards, these images of Dragons seemed to be flying directly towards the battlefield. If you listened closely, it sounded as if they were roaring. Then, I could see hundreds of beams fall from the heavens directly onto where our defensive line was.

Mother dropped her stance and turned around, there was a subtle expression of exhaustion upon Mother's face, "**That**, young Draxfur, is the true strength the Gods bestow upon us!"

As Mother turned to us, I noticed her eyes were glowing, but they were slowly returning to normal. Steam was emitting from her hands, and the emblems were fading away. At this time in my life, I had not yet witnessed such immense magic, certainly not this close, and definitely not from my Mother. Her energy levels were immeasurable but were now fading back to normal.

Draxfur was too left in astonishment, just as I was. I knew of my Mother's strength, but that was beyond what my young mind thought it to be. As Mother was taking up her posture, I could sense love within her heart, as if the power that was unleashed was a direct reflection of that in which she holds for our kin. Such powerful and unconditional love.

"Let us follow the innocent, young Draxfur. Please fly with me until our army and my husband return to us," Mother asked as she claimed me within her arms once again.

"Yes M'Lady!" Draxfur responded while arming himself with his mystical bow.

As the Warriors of our army retreated, so did we. Mother and Draxfur leapt off the ridge with no fear, free falling towards the ocean's fierce morning waves and then spreading their wings to catch flight. The feeling of the air moving around us was as refreshing as it was exhilarating. Soaring over the open seas, there is truly nothing like it.

Mother was quick on land and through the skies. She looked back at Draxfur with a humorous smile on her face as she watched him try to catch up. The worry that I felt within her heart was no longer there. She slowed her pace so that Draxfur may be able to reach us.

"**So**, *Draxfur of the Mountains*, until my War Chief returns and we reach the masses of our pack, tell me of your story, of your name," Mother ever so curiously inquired.

"M'Lady, with all due respect, *I do not believe now is the time for acquaintance*?" Draxfur questionably replied.

"Now is better a time than ever. How else am I supposed to tell my husband of the Scout who stuck by my side ever so faithfully?" Mother insisted.

Draxfur seemed a bit confused. We had just witnessed a battle occur, the heavens were split, and our kin was running from the dangers that follow. Yet Mother was insistent on knowing whom this Scout was. On making general, and off the topic, casual conversation. Although he did not understand how Mother was not concerned for what was ahead, he obliged.

"M'Lady, my name is that of my own. A simple name I heard in the streets when I was young, so I claimed it for myself. I am of my own kin and have never known my own blood, abandoned before eyes first sight," Draxfur told my Mother, with his heart weighted heavily.

"Continue young Scout. You are amongst one of concern and there is nothing but time," Mother carefully suggested.

"I fended for myself within the mountains when a group of Scouts came across me. I knew nothing of this world, and the Scouts of this clan took me in as their own. They raised me and turned me into the best of Scouts that I can be. It is all I have ever known and all I will ever want." Draxfur said with pride in his words.

"Surely you want a family of your own one day, maybe to trade your bow for a blade, or maybe even retire your bow and be one of knowledge rather than battle?" Mother continued questioning Draxfur.

"With all respects to scholars and Warriors, M'Lady, I only ever wish to continue being a Scout. To be the best that I can be for those who truly brought me into this world." Draxfur responded.

Mother and Draxfur continued conversing until eventually the masses of our pack were in distance of our sight. Luckily, our enemies had not predicted our entire movement so there was no ambush awaiting us in the great seas. Joyful cheering rose from ahead of us once the pack discovered-Mother's return.

Once we were at the head of the pack, Mother informed the others that we could now slow our pace to conserve energy. That the defense of our retreat was successful and that the remainder of our pack would return to us shortly. Everyone was enlightened to hear that news. It was almost visible; the weight that left the hearts of those around.

Draxfur stuck with us until Mother noticed him looking down at the rest of the Scouts. After hearing his story, his trials and tribulations, Mother knew that the Scouts were the only family that he had. That all he would ever want to be is a Scout, with his family.

"Draxfur, if you wish to return with your comrades, you may do so with no disrespect to us. We will be fine waiting for the others. Do not feel like you are unwanted or being a burden by our side, because your company is truly honored," Mother gracefully spoke.

"*Are you sure M'Lady*? I am fine by your side until the War Chief returns." Draxfur responded.

"**Go, be with your brothers at arms**! We will be fine. Thank you Draxfur, for the shared company and words!" Mother replied.

Draxfur was hesitant at first, he maybe thought this to be a double-edged sword, that it may in fact be a test of his loyalty. Mother assured him that we would be fine, and that his presence was most likely missed by his brothers.

Draxfur was thankful towards Mother and saluted her before he dropped his flight pattern to match that of his brothers. We could see them talking to him and pointing towards us. The possibility of their curiosities raised, due to his time spent with our clan's Shield Maiden. Mother chuckled for a moment and then continued guiding our clan South through the seas.

Just before the sun met the dawning horizon, we could hear the victory cries of our army. The cheerful laughter between Warriors filled the air. It was a glorious sight. Hundreds of Warriors flying in formation together, still armed to the teeth and decorated in their magnificent armor.

Father was leading them, and it did not seem as if their numbers were short. They soon caught up to the masses that Mother was leading. Fathers, Brothers, Husbands, and lovers all finding those whom they fought for. I could sense hearts being restored with the sight of their loved one returning.

"**My love!**" my Father joyfully shouted as he dashed forward to us. Just before he reached us, the sun had set in the distance.

"*What did I tell you*!?" Mother snickered.

"**You have told me many things over our lifespan!**" Father humorously replied.

"*I told you that I expected you by my side before the days last light*, **did I not**!?" Mother questioned with cleverness and appeared angry.

"*But....*" Father tried explaining himself before Mother cut him off,

"**No**, ***the heavens were my witness to such words, and they have never held anything but integrity!***" Mother shouted.

Silence was casted over us, and Father had the most confused look on his face. Mother could not hold her angry face much longer, she soon after erupted with laughter. A gasp of relief came from Father, and he soon joined her in rejoice. As everything and everyone were becoming settled with such a vast reunion, it seemed all was well.

"My love, all humor and rejoice aside, without you taking the risk of tapping into your natural magical abilities, this army would have not returned. This enemy that is after us, they are nothing we have ever faced before. *Even with such a defense, still some were lost.*" Father confessed.

After Father stated that, Mother could not help but to look around. Through all the rejoice, there were few with the look of despair, the look that proved their loved ones had fallen. Tears were rolling down the cheeks of those who held their loved ones for the last time.

"*We must not ponder on that in which leads our mind into darkness. We must yet breathe life into these young ones and secure the future that is promised,*" Mother reassured.

"You speak wisdom, M'Lady, yet I fear this power that attempts to consume us will not allow a promised new age," Father deeply graved.

During our tiring flight over the great sea, Father talked more of the battle, and of the enemy that sought our lives. He continued to proclaim how much Mother was a vital role in their survival, that without her, many more lives may had been claimed.

Mother wished to get Father's mind from the battle and told him of the faithful Scout Draxfur, of the confidence that she had in such a faithful Scout. She asked that he be trained as a Warrior once we arrived at the Twelve Kingdoms. That maybe the words of a War Chief could move such a young heart and mind into further progressing his position in life. To become more than he sees himself to be.

So, Father promised that once all lives were secured under the skies within the Twelve Kingdoms, he would seek out this Draxfur and oblige Mother's request. Even with Mother's reassuring words I could sense there was still caution within Father's heart, that nothing else occupied his mind, other than this enemy at our heels.

CHAPTER NINE
WORDS WITHIN WHISPERING WINDS

Still so young and oblivious to the actual concept of life. Still unaware of how time was utterly understood. I counted time as the sun and moon rose and fell. This was my understanding, the way I viewed the sands of time passing through the hourglass.

The sun had risen and stretched across the horizon many times over our journey. The moon had reached those same distant perspectives just as frequently. It was but only on a night in which the moon was creeping over the seemingly endless stretch of Oceans around us. When we vaguely sighted land through the moon and starlit fogs. The spirits within those whom witnessed this had begun to rise.

Father knew this journey was yet over. Without calling the formation to a halt verbally, he signaled for everyone to slow their pace and hold their positions. Father extended his hands and his aura flickered. As I peered around, I noticed the Warriors of higher prestige begin to draw their own auras as well. Cautious of what was ahead, Father knew that hasty action should not be taken, that no matter how promising the sight may be, there is always reason to be wary.

I noticed there was always a representative from each section of the fighting forces closely positioned near Father. I could only assume that they were the Commanders for their individual sections. Upon coming to a hovering halt, Father motioned towards one of these individuals.

"Aurumscale, come closer." Father waved to the nearby Scout Commander.

Aurumscale, first of his name, last of his kin. Illustrious green vines seemed to emerge from his back and were wrapped around his wings. Thick and sharpened thorns coated his wings endlessly. That which should be leathery between seemed to be thickened leaves, coated with a poisonous essence. His eyes were mirrored images of luscious emerald fields. He was decorated in the pelt of what seemed to be a mythical beast.

"Yes, my Chief?" Aurumscale replied ever so quietly.

"As Commander of the Scouting masses, know I want a forward Scouting party to conduct some reconnaissance on that incoming land mass. Take with you the bare minimum and do so with careful but considerable haste," Father ordered.

"Your word is Command, my Chief!" Aurumscale answered and then swiftly dashed towards the Scouting formations.

Upon Aurumscale's arrival to his respective formation, I witnessed short conversation between him and a few highly decorated Warriors. Soon after, a small section of those Scouts broke from their positions and began readying themselves for travel. Aurumscale was following Fathers orders as directed and was putting together the Scouting party.

"Draxralin." Father waved to another nearby Commander.

"I have already got a few in mind, my Chief!" Draxralin, the Tower Shields Commander, replied.

Draxralin, War Chief of wars past and former Chief to a forgotten clan. This brute of a Warrior did not yield one, but two massive claymores. Both the pommels of these savage beams of steel burnt redder than the suns core. There was an ancient feel to these blades, and even rested you could sense mysterious energies emitting from the very edges of his savage weaponry.

Draxralin was quick to his own formation as well. He handpicked only six Tower Shields. Once they were selected, these Dragokin knew they were soon to meet the minority of Scouts who were waiting nearby. Once all were together, they dashed in the direction of the nearby lands we had spotted.

"Your people are tired, my Love. Holding this position may cause for catastrophic exhaustion in some," Mother said concerningly to Father.

"I know this, but to ask the same people to descend within an unfamiliar land may be asking them to sign their own death sentence. We must remain vigilant; we must remain cautious," Father said as he broke from our side and soared through the formations.

My eyes swayed from Father to the four Commanders who flew directly towards our Armies section of the hovering masses. I noticed, one by one, Father and the Commanders were selecting Dragokin from the Warriors. Each Warrior that was handpicked soon broke from their positions and began to conduct aid and assist those within our pack. As I snuggled tighter into Mother's own exhausted arms, my heart began to feel for those who seemed to be losing what strength remained.

Father was not considered a Leader for his strength alone. He was not chosen as War Chief for that of his knowledge alone either. He was carefully and considerably chosen because his leadership surpassed all that in which was written in the tomes. He did not order unless he himself was up for the task. Even in his Fatherhood, he was never afraid to kick up his own dust and flail his own wings, teaching by example, especially during simpler times when it came to teaching me how to play childhood games.

As I was cradled within Mother's arms, she was soon to break from the lead of our formation as well. As we too flew through the masses of our pack, I was able to closely witness the truly tiresome expressions upon the faces of those all around. Father surely was not exaggerating the intensity of the vast seas. He spoke of true concern, navigating the open oceans, yet we were presented no other options. It was to survive or die trying.

Although we ran into no issues from Bundok ng Dragon thus far, the flight alone had taken what little breath every Dragokin within our crowds yet yielded. I noticed as well that our numbers had been reduced again. Although there were great strengths of power flying all around me, there was also great exhaustion. One did not need to count to know that there were some who did not make it.

As I continued scanning the crowds, I noticed some of our kin hanging around the shoulders of those with more strength than themselves. Mostly the young, those who were too large to be cradled like myself. Prideful beings we Dragokin are, so therefore I was not surprised if there were some who chose to be claimed by the seas.

Mother continued through the crowds, questioning the health and sanity of those around, ensuring that strength still fuels the fire within everyone's hearts. We were soon to approach the lead of our masses again. Mother was slowing her flight and hovered nearby a crowd of Dragokin that looked much like the Royal Guards, except, these Dragokin did not wear gold plated armor. It was as if their wings and scales themselves were forged with the purest of gold, their eyes resembling streams of liquid gold flowing ever so gently.

"*Artana, how is your child?*" Mother asked as she neared the woman she called for.

"**He is strong**, *even that surpassed of his Fathers strength, and* **he will survive**," the woman with magnificent golden shimmering wings replied.

"*There is land nearby, I have been reminding all those around that our path has been lit by Hengtuin himself. We* **must finish this through**!" Mother spoke with courage.

"**With the flames of destiny lit, we shall follow those who wield the torch**!" Artana responded before Mother pushed towards the lead of our pack.

Father was not far behind us in regaining the lead of the formation. *"Our numbers have surely dropped since our departure, but all those that were lost did so under their own will. They fought for as long as they could, but this ongoing battle had just become too much, my Love."*

"Hengtuin will guide those lost souls, as he continues to guide us," Mother responded.

"If these lands are proven to be safe, we must cast fire over the seas and conduct memorials for those that we have lost." Father explained to Mother, and if not closely observing Father, you would have missed the subtle display of deepened pain.

"No truer words have been spoken." Mother solemnly agreed.

It was not long that we waited there for the return of the Scouting party. However, it was a shock when only one Scout returned. There was no look of concern pasted across his face, and no signs of battle. As the Scout began to approach Father, he stopped momentarily. The Scout drew an arrow from his quiver and sparked it with his very flame. The light this emitted was immaculate through the night's fog. His hand began to illuminate as he readied the arrow, and then off into the night's sky he sent it.

We just watched as the flaming arrow climbed through the sky, growing smaller, and glowing duller, until it finally vanished. Soon after, it burst with flames and with it, in the distance, fires began to stretch across the land masses edge. One by one, it was as if great pyres were set to flames, which began to light what we now noticed to be a coast.

My eyes widened to this marvelous sight. We were still so far away, yet it seemed as if we could feel the very heart of those flames. Warming our flesh that has been chilled over the open oceans. Breaking the ice from our cold hearts and restoring faith within our shivering souls.

"War Chief, the lands are clear and secured for landing!" the Scout proclaimed as he approached Father with a courteous salute.

Hearing such words echoing through the crowds led there to be an intense wave of anticipation, anxiousness. I could feel not only Mother's and Father's hearts, but all those around began to widen their eyes and flutter their wings with even just a bit more strength. As I was peeking over Mother's shoulder, I saw the eyes of hundreds finding their own sights upon us.

"Good, let us make haste towards these lands and guide those of our pack within a secure perimeter. We must catch breath before this journey continues!" Father ordered and the Scout obliged.

The Scout bowed and was quick towards the fighting masses of our pack. Upon his arrival, it seemed there was not a moment to spare before there was widespread motion. The leads of these formations began ordering the fighting forces to move forward. In their own individual sections, Warriors began to fly hastily towards the fire engulfed shores. Other individuals from the fighting forces broke from the forward assault. It seemed they were adding to the bolstering numbers that were already assisting those who were on the edge of catastrophic exhaustion.

From this stand still hovering position, our pack moved desperately behind the Warriors, allowing them to continue serving as our people's shield. As we continued to push forward, and through the clearing of the fog, sight of dry land began to fill everyone with hope. We all followed closely behind the fighting forces, allowing them to land first to begin securing and settling within these new lands.

Finally, our hearts and everyone's strength could be restored. Through observation, these foreign islands were spread vastly, and there were many to be found. Further in the distance was a much larger land mass. As our pack began to find ground and descend from the skies, I noticed the Warriors from our pack had already begun to establish bunkered positions scattered throughout the isles. It seemed they were completely thoughtless with setting up defenses, as if this were a first nature to these beasts. They were leaving open areas in the middle of their defenses for the civilians of our pack to settle within.

"**My Chief**," Aurumscale begun while approaching Father, "*My Scouts have reason to believe we have reached the Lomarin Islands. The geographical features of this coastline represent that much like Lomarin.*"

"*If this is to be so, we were not set off trail through the Great Seas and this is enlightening news. Have you already set forth a forward Scouting party to continue reconnaissance on these lands?*" Father replied.

"*I have put together the Scouting party, but we await your command, **my Chief**.*" Aurumscale urged.

"**This is why you have been selected as Commander my good friend**. Before you set motion forward, bring the Scout by the name of Draxfur to me," Father ordered.

"Yes, my Chief!" Aurumscale saluted Father before dashing towards the Scouting masses of our pack.

"**SCOUT DRAXFUR, REPORT**!" Aurumscale shouted over his shoulder towards his Scouts.

Soon after, there he was, Draxfur of the Mountains. The Scout that assisted Mother before we fled our lands. He rushed through the crowds that were preparing the camps, bow readily in his hand and hood veiled over his face. He bowed before his Commander and was ordered to report to Father.

"**Yes, War Chief**?" Draxfur asked as he approached us while kneeling before Father's presence.

"M'Lady speaks highly of you, young Scout. I not only wanted to give you my personal gratitude for being there by her side, but I also want to appoint you lead of this Scouting mission. **Prove yourself to me now young Scout!**" Father boasted.

"**Your words are my command, War Chief!**" Draxfur responded before saluting Father and returning to a group of Scouts that were finishing preparations for movement.

     Once Father gave the Scouts the signal to proceed, they dashed towards the larger Island with remarkable speed. As I have seen before, there were few Warriors that followed closely to the Scouts. I had begun to realize this seemed to be a custom for our people. Everything Dragokin do must be done so with regards to the older customs. It keeps tradition in order and allows us to always remember the success of the past.

     Once the Commanders of each fighting section were finished ordering their masses, they began to set a camp separate of those from our pack, with the few that were selected from their own masses to see to the task. Even without being ordered by Father, these Commanders knew what was to follow upon landing within these islands.

"My Love, I must sit with the Commanders and Elders to discuss our next move. Be sure our people get the rest that is desperately needed. As Shield Maiden your command is just as mine," Father said to Mother just before he dashed towards the Commanders camp.

"Your Father's mind flies more hastily than suns new light greeting land, my Dragon," Mother whispered to me as she too began to make camp amongst our clan.

As the night aged, our kin were finally setting their heads to rest and falling into a much-needed slumber. The Warriors in our pack stood vigilantly so that those who needed to, may rest. Mother did not set us to bed. She stood as well, until every Dragokin in our pack was finally able to rest.

Mother began walking towards the Commanders camp where we could see the leaders of our clan sitting around a subtle fire. Each of these Warriors, I had seen before. Decorated so brilliantly, shields and weaponry set readily available at their sides. The fire's light danced ever so gently across their own vicious appearances. Before Mother fully approached, Father looked over to us and waved us to accompany him.

"**Sit with us my Love**, we are just finished discussing politics." Father said to Mother as he patted the ground in front of him.

"If you boys are finished with my Chief, I would ask that I may now discuss *politics* with him as well, **alone**," Mother snickered.

The Commanders amongst our presence had begun to chuckle amongst themselves. They sensed the intense sarcasm in Mother's tone just as I did. One by one they stood,

"May Hengtuin himself offer you Protection from what is to come my Chief!" Aurumscale stated while saluting Father and finding himself away from the fire.

"The shadows themselves have no concealment for you on this night my Chief," Another Commander stated before disseminating into a darkened fog which disappeared into the shadows.

"I have got faith in you brother; I have fought alongside the Shield Maiden, and I do not side with the cowardly! **Give er' hell**!" Draxralin said humorously while patting Father's shoulder, "**Prydlorik**, let's join our men for friendly sparring!"

"Do not listen to him my Chief, we all know these are battles not to be considered because they will be far from won!" the fourth Commander, Prydlorik chuckled to Father while saluting him.

Once the Commanders presence were no longer within earshot, Mother just stood there and glared at Father. It was as if she knew there was something that Father never discussed with her. That there was a secret hiding deep within his mind.

"*My Love*...." Father pleaded.

"**Do not** *my Love,* **me**. What are the *politics* you have yet to discuss with **me**?" Mother said furiously.

"These politics have yet to be discussed with anyone. I stated our path was lit, but the exact whereabouts and routes of this path have only been set within my mind and my mind alone," Father claimed.

"*Hmmm*, and **what** is it that *ponders* within my Love's mind?" Mother urged.

"*If my words reached these lands, we should have safe passage across the island and our path safely set directly towards the Twelve Kingdoms,*" Father explained to Mother.

"Our clan has no connections with Lomarin Island. *How could you have achieved sending word here?*" Mother replied with a bit of anger.

"*There was but one name I heard rumors of living here. An old friend and brother at arms. There are many Dragokin clans here and I can only hope those rumors were true,*" Father explained.

"Who is it that you believe to be here? You never spoke to me about such a plan," Mother questioned.

"The less that could be easily heard, the better. With how much has happened we do not know where the winds carry our words, even in private," Father replied.

The look of anger soon fell from Mother's face. She glanced around to the masses of our kin. She now understood Father's secrecy, that a plan known within one mind cannot be easily breached or predicted. Mother was soon to set us between Father's legs, and she leaned back into his lap.

"If you believe in your heart that you made the right decision then, as always, I will forever stand by your words...." Mother whispered, as she then began humming a sweet tune.

CHAPTER TEN
YOU ARE NOW CHIEF

As *I found myself deep within the dream realm, I was in yet another dark room. This time, I was an apparition of my current self, viewing the body of what I began to assume was my future self. That or another Dragokin that portrayed remarkably similar traits to that of myself.*

There were ancient symbols painted on the ground, meticulously arranged in a circle. Each of these symbols were a different color of the spectrum. The symbol this older Dragokin, this Dragokin that has begun appearing within my dreams, was lying unconsciously upon, was the archaic symbol that was painted **Gray**.

The nine remaining symbols; **Black**, **White**, **Red**, **Violet**, **Blue**, **Green**, **Yellow**, *and* **Orange**. *All these symbols were empty. There were no bodies that laid unconscious upon them. Only the Gray symbol. Only the Dragokin that I have been seeing within my slumber. He is the only one that was within this room.*

Soon after, the ancient Gray symbol slowly began to illuminate. Then, within this symbol enlightened aura, smoke begun to form a perfect barrier around the unconscious body of this Dragokin. I attempted to shout out, anything, but nothing was mustered between mind and tongue.

*As this smoke continued to grow thicker, the systematically graphed symbol grew brighter. "**DRAGO**!" was beginning to chant within this empty room. The darkness around me was thick. There were no other souls to be sought, however, many voices were heard within the chant. Some of those voices feeling familiar to my heart and ears.*

Soon after the voices had faded, I witnessed the familiar Dragokin begin to float in the air above the symbol in which he was bound. Not only the smoke, but this brilliant light as well, began to whirl around in tandem. His eyes had opened widely, and his mouth was gaping as the smoke and light began to infiltrate his body.

*"**DRAGO**!" was once again heard, this time shouted within the abyss of this room.*

Once the room fell silent again, so did the body of this Dragokin. Slowly he descended as the last bit of smoke and light filled his very being. He seemed to be conscious now, just kneeling in the solitude of this silence. Then, he quickly glanced back towards me, and our eyes made direct contact with one another.

*"**REMEMBER**!" he shouted.*

My eyes once again cracked the seal of the slumber I was subdued within. Mother and Father laid next to me as the day's new light was breaking the distant horizon. Mother felt as my heart rattled, and my eyes curiously set upon the world. She too was awakened by my actions.

"**My Dragon**, *what is it that startles your young heart?*" Mother whispered and she returned me within her loving and nurturing grip, "*What has my Dragon so immensely shook upon this day?*"

I just looked Mother in the eyes and gripped onto her arm firmly. Still, there were no words to be mustered. No answer for her beckoning questions. It was as if there was no need. Mother's eyes read mine and with such she replied, "*You mustn't worry young Drago, for your kin lights a righteous path to walk upon!*"

As Mother finished cradling me closer to her, Father rolled closer to us and asked, "*Why has my flesh and blood risen so early?*"

"*It is nothing my Love, though now presents it possible to continue our path towards the Twelve Kingdoms,*" Mother replied.

"*If my Shield Maiden speaks it,* **then it must be true**," Father whispered as he began to shake his own slumber from mind.

Mother and Father began to waken themselves, and all those around were following suit. There was not much time for such pleasantries and the path ahead was still immense. Father was soon to gather the Commanders to further our trail from our enemies.

"**Aurumscale! Gather your men and begin to push through these lands, lighting us a path towards the opposing coast!**"

"**Yes, my Chief!**" Aurumscale replied and then began to order the Scouts to begin movement.

"My Love, I am to check on Artana and the remaining Shield Maidens!" Mother said to Father before breaking from his side.

Mother began to walk through the crowds of tiresome Dragokin. One by one they bowed before Mother's presence as she passed. She begged of them to reserve their energy for the coming path and reminded them that their retreat is still top of priority.

"**Artana**! I see you are breathing strength within all those around!" Mother said as she approached the golden winged Dragokin.

"We are all kin within these ranks, so whatever we must do to ensure our safe retreat!" Artana replied as she finished handing out food to those moving with the masses.

"We believe us to be upon the Lomarin Islands, I mustn't speak much upon what is to come but our path should be shielded within these lands," Mother said as she closer approached this woman.

I was soon to notice the Hatchling that Artana was carrying just as Mother was with me. Ever so preciously, with her utmost guard. He was sleeping soundlessly within his Mother's arms and covered himself with his wings.

"So long as our people and our children escape the grasps of our enemies, our own lives are not to be placed upon the same scales!" Artana replied as the remaining Shield Maidens in earshot tapped their swords against their shields.

"You have always spoken wisdom and have always proved the strongest of love!" Mother was soon to finish as she embraced Artana with a firm hug.

Beyond my own ears reach, even being hairs away from Mothers lips to Artana's ears, something was whispered. Something so subtle that not even the winds carried a hint of what was said. After their embrace, Mother stared deeply within Artana's eyes.

Afterward, Mother began to make her way towards where she left Father and the Commanders. At this point, everyone was ready for the next move. Still bearing tiresome looks upon their faces, still breathing heavily as breath has not yet been fully caught. Our people needed to continue no matter the cost.

Father stood at the lead of the pack with the remaining Commanders. All the Scouts that were ordered to move were in the distance as the sun began to break the horizon. Father turned around as we began to approach them and said, **"Let us continue, my Love!"**

    The night in which I was separated from my pack is a series of images burned within my memory. I was merely a hatchling; I was unable to walk unassisted or even speak. It was the blood and tears that flowed on that fatal day that will never be forgotten.

    Through the clouds, streams of sunlight guided our flight path. A calm breeze brushed my cheeks as we glided towards these new land's main beach. The day was young, and this journey was far from over. After reaching the mainland we began to hover over an evergreen forest.

    Rain began to fall heavily from the skies. There was a thick, dampened fog that also began to form around us. The winds started slow, but soon began to find their own violent speeds. Little did anyone know; this was only the beginning.

"Where are the Scouts, I sent forward!?" Father questioned the nearby Commanders.

"This fog has only been birthed as of recently my Chief, there is no way Aurumscale, and his men have already found themselves lost within it!" Draxralin replied and was soon to push a small group of Tower Shields forward to find the Scouts.

"**Either your words were heard by the wrong ears, or the Scouts have landed elsewhere. Let us remain hidden within the clouds just to be sure, my Love,**" Mother suggested.

I was held firmly within Mother's arms. Father was next to us, and the rest of our pack followed behind. I could sense the trust in which our pack placed within Father. Other than Mother, he was the strongest Dragokin amongst us. I could not imagine anyone else being the leader of my kin, my blood.

"He has got your eyes," Father insisted as he flew closer to us.

"That may be true, but he has a beating heart much like yours," Mother replied.

"When he comes of age to wield a blade, I shall be the one to determine that!" Father boasted while tapping his chest with his fist.

"What if he does not wish to wield a blade?" Mother snickered.

"**He is a son of Hengtuin! The art of battle burns within him!**" Father shouted with joy.

"**DRAGO!**" the Warriors of our Pack cried out.

Mother and Father shared laughter. Tears of joy filled Mother's beautiful silver eyes. I did not understand why they were laughing, though I could not resist letting out a chuckle myself. I could tell Mother adored my laughter.

Soon after, Father held his hand up and ordered everyone to stop. The joy which was on his face was now a stern look. Such a look that reignited the fire in his eyes, much like I have seen upon his face before battles of the past.

Father observed the forest floor below us and keenly listened beyond the fluttering of our pack's wings. There was not much to be seen beyond the fog that was now beginning to thin, and not much to be heard beyond the howling winds that were beginning to calm. Father thought there to be otherwise.

Father signaled for the Warriors of our pack to drop their flight posture into a defensive formation. The Warriors drew their weapons and shields and took up a protective flight posture below and around those who were innocent within our pack. Father, now drawing his own blades and mustering his magical abilities, had a deep red aura consuming his body.

"*What is it my love?*" Mother asked as she flew closer to Father.

"**Do you hear that?**" Father questioned.

Battle cries had begun to emerge from below us. Then, flame engulfed arrows began to flood the skies. These were not normal flames, much different than an inferno from Dragon's breath. These flames were dark green with streams of black flowing through them. I had seen these flames before, used by the enemies that hunted us.

Trivial numbers within our pack suffered fatal injuries from this assaulting barrage against us. The flaming arrows pierced through those wearing little to no armor, forcing the life out of them as they plummeted from the sky. The dark green flames consumed their bodies as they fiercely cried out their last words.

Father acted quickly, pointing in the direction of a nearby plain and ordering everyone to rush there. The innocent and unarmed within our pack flew in the direction of the plain. The Warriors were holding their defensive posture while slowly following, attempting to cut down and shield as many arrows as they could. It seemed as if the arrows had no end. Although the Warriors were acting as a shield from the arrows, more of my kin had fallen.

It was a gruesome sight to witness. Dragokin are supposed to be immune to flames because we emerged from the mystical and ancient Dragons themselves. Yet these green flames were evil. They burned through those that were pierced as easily as paper to a flame, searing their flesh from their bones, only leaving trails of ashes in their wake.

Mother flew towards Father and shouted, "**You mustn't face them! Not here! Not now! Escape with us!**"

"You know they will continue to find us if we are not to make a stand **here and now! We are so close!** This is the only way to ensure the remainder of our pack lives!" Father shouted just before cutting down a few arrows that were intended for Mother.

"**There has to be ano**........." Mother shouted as Father was quick to wrapping her within his arms.

Whilst between them in this embrace, I felt both of their heartbeats. Father's pounding for war. Mothers in distress. Both their bodies tense, as if they wanted to freeze time itself and never leave this moment. To finally end all the madness and just live within this still instant.

Father interrupted her, "Lead the innocent and unarmed of our pack to safety. See to it that the prophecy is fulfilled and ensure the young ones do not draw their last breath! **I am still the leader of this pack, you are still a Shield Maiden, and this is an order!**"

With slight hesitation, Mother's posture changed. Mother's beautiful silver eyes became filled with endless tears. Soon they began to glow gray. Her body illuminated, and her wings spread wide. She quickly turned while sheltering me within her arms.

As Father ordered, Mother acted. One powerful thrust with Mother's wings and we were headed in the direction in which Father first ordered for all to retreat toward. We noticed the retreating formations of our pack nearing the plain in which they were ordered to land.

Before we achieved such a distance from out of eyesight, I glanced down towards the origins of the arrows. I was soon to bear witness again to these savage dwarves who carried red clan banners. They were faint blurs from high above. As my eyes focused, I could see their long-braided beards, faces painted with blood, and their red clan banners that portrayed a cracked dragon skull in the middle.

I could hear Father's strong voice still, even as we drew our distance, "**Protect those we love with our very breath! Allow none to fall to these cowards! Brothers, this is where we put an end to these honorless bastards!**"

As all were beginning to land within the concealment of the tree line, Mother was soon to regain control of our pack. As we descended upon the forest floor, all those around were looking towards Mother. Mother's eyes still obvious with tears, our entire pack trembled before Mother's own heartbreaking glance.

"Fear not, for our path has yet to be doused. There is still hope that our pack may breathe life. What has come and what still waits ahead have and will become scars that mark your story! For now, more so than ever, I am asking that you push your very life to the limits so that we all may live beyond this nightmare!" Mother shouted in hopes to restore faith into the hearts of our people.

"What are we to do M'Lady?" one voice shouted.

"There is little to no life in most M'Lady!" another voice shouted.

There was endless chatter and panic within the ranks of our people. Mother hoped to restore allegiance in those around. She hoped that her words may provide strength, that her aura may seep into all around so that they may escape. But the panic continued, and I felt Mother's heart weaken from the thought that she had failed.

"**STOP!**" a familiar voice shouted as I noticed a pathway being created through the crowds.

It was Artana, the golden winged Dragokin that Mother seemed to be so fond with, "**We are Dragokin! We were born for battle, bathed in blood, and our hearts forged with fire! We mustn't stop until there proves to be no life remaining within our bodies and souls!**"

"Artana...." Mother said in her own silence as Artana continued towards Mother.

"**Quisvale is your Shield Maiden! Her love and guidance alone has guided this entire pack from darkness! Allow her to speak!**" Artana said as she bowed before Mother.

"*Artana, please! Find your ground!* **Rise as the Shield Maiden you have always been as well!**" Mother said as she gripped Artana's arm.

"**Forgive us M'Lady!**" voices within the crowds began to muster.

"Do not believe you have dishonored me, because we are living within trying times! Do not believe my faith within your hearts has faltered, because I still yet feel your faith within mine!" Mother shouted, "We must give this retreat our everything, or I fear our everything will be taken from all! Conceal your scents with the mud around! Break from everything that might burden your pace! Retreat through this forest and do not look back!"

Now. Now I felt Mother's words pierce through the very hearts of all those around. Everyone within earshot obeyed Mother's orders. Quickly coating themselves with mud, dropping all that in which weighed them to Nydeli's surface, and without hesitation. They conjured what strength and life they had within them to continue retreating opposite of where our Warriors held ground.

"Quisvale, do not let me witness you too far behind. I know where your heart currently stands, because mine would be bound to the same!" Artana said to Mother just before following the retreating numbers.

Mother stood for a moment to ensure the innocent all made retreat, soon after she turned to see our Warriors slowly retreating towards us. As the endless barrage of arrows continued filling the air of the battlefield, the Warriors continued shielding them from reaching us. The wall of Dragokin Warriors was faultless. The most skilled Warriors in all the lands. Different auras illuminating from their bodies, fearlessly defending those they love.

Mother rushed through the masses of Warriors to find Father. Once we finally found him Mother broke him from the rage of war and pleaded, "**You do not have to do this! None of you do! We have survived this far already!**"

"The more we delay the prophecy, the more we risk our future! **Leave, now**! **Guide the pack**! Save as many as possible and ensure the young ones survive, if not anyone else!" Father replied with rage, I could sense the rage was not towards Mother. It was the rage of war.

I could also sense the heartbreak Mother was now suffering from. As if a piece of her own heart shattered before our eyes and faded into the sky. Father placed his hand upon her cheek and gave her a passionate kiss. He removed an ancient pendant from around his neck. This pendant hung from a heavy obsidian chain. Father then draped it around my own neck. He placed his hand upon my cheek and joined my eyes in an endless gaze. This was the first time I ever witnessed Father cry.

"**I, Charmortus Gray-Flame**, underneath the heavens and in front of my blood, **relinquish my title as Chief! I now appoint Quisvale Gray-Flame as Chief of the Dragon's Blood Clan!**" Father shouted as he cut his palm and painted an ancient symbol of blood on Mother's face. Then, Father pierced his blades into the muds beneath and began to unwrap two riddled sashes that were knotted around his bulging biceps.

"**DRAGO!**" all the Warriors from our pack shouted. Father began wrapping one sash around Mother's arm, and the other he draped around my shoulders as a cape would hang, sophistically knotted in a triangular design.

"**No! You will not accept this as your fate!**" Mother screamed, tears flooding heavily from her eyes and her voice trembling.

"With this very emblem, from the days of old, let it bear **my Title, my Heart, my Soul!**" Father continued.

"**DRAGO**!" The Warriors plead still thundering in the background, the roaring clatter of magnificent beings preparing for battle, melodizing songs of war.

"**NO! CHARMORTUS**!" Mother shouted as she pounded Father's breastplate with her fist. Begging, pleading, attempting to break his words from continuation.

"From this day forth, until this symbol is relinquished, may you guide her under your very wings!" Father finished. His deeply reddened eyes finding mine, glistening as his own tears formed within.

Father then placed his head against Mothers. Their tears falling where we stood, dancing together within their red and gray auras, *"As Chief you must lead our kin away from danger my love,* **this you cannot avoid. Now go,** *this is my last order as your former Chief and forever love......"* Father whispered with passion as his hands cradled Mothers tear covered cheeks.

"*But...*" Mother whispered through her trembling lips, through her fractured heart, and broken words.

"*Our souls have been intertwined; our love has been unbreakable!* **For I will find you within the heavens and love you once again!**" Father said as he slowly released his grips around Mother. Looking to me once more with his tear-soaked eyes, Father turned from us without retuning his saddening sights.

"If this is to be our last day to breathe life, brothers, let us make it a battle to be sung over the ages!" Father shouted as his aura pulsed and stirred up dust.

"**DRAGO!**" the Warriors shouted again while slamming their magnificent weapons and antiquated shields together. I could feel their pride swell through the crowd like the ocean ebbs at high tide. I too felt my core swell. With pride. With grief. With shock.

"**Let our enemies remember that no matter their numbers, we did not falter!**" Father shouted as his magical aura became greater. Father's fingers systematically graphed patterns in thin air. As if he were breaking the fabrics of Nature to paint these darkened illuminations.

"**DRAGO!**" the Warriors replied with their own auras growing. Some were removing pieces of armor, praising the Gods they followed, wagering battlefield accomplishments.

"**That no matter the lives claimed on this day, we still live on!**" Father continued while rallying the Commanders to his side. Those faces that in which I have become so familiar with. Truly savage beings that stood within Nydeli. Their powers, and strengths, remarkable.

"**DRAGO!**"

"**It has been an honor to be your Chief, your brother at arms, and your kin**! If you wish to turn now to secure your own survival with those you love, you will not be stopped nor dishonored! Allow the heavens to claim you on your own decision and not mine!" Father ended before drawing his own magical blades again, forcing their edges to whistle, becoming fully consumed in a dark red and gray aura, not only his blades, but his entire being.

"**BROTHER! You have bled long enough for us! Let this song of death and blood honor all of our names!**" Draxralin shouted as he rallied the Tower Shields. Brutely savage Dragokin wielding massive claymores and battle axes. Fierce spears and deadly halberds. All finding their position shadowing Father's.

"Now that he is not **Chief**, we do not have to make him look good upon the honor of the battlefield!" Prydlorik followed with the Twin Blades. Each of these merciless Dragokin juggling or spinning fearsome axes, or blood-stained blades. Harnessing physical energies that would seem to never be matched.

"*The shadows of the battlefield shall decide where our fate lies, **my Chief**!*" said the Commander of the shadows as he seeped from Nydeli's surface. Then, hundreds, or what seemed to be thousands, of Shadows began hauntingly rising from the grounds beneath us. Their smoky aura waving in the winds, menacing laughter echoing and creaking around us.

From such a response, I gathered that none of the Warriors considered Father's proposal of turning and retreating. Every Dragokin Warrior, decorated in gold trimmed obsidian armor, armed to the teeth with mystical weapons, mirrored my Father's actions. A brute wall of the most skilled Warriors in the world lined up next to Father. Each Warrior giving off a different colored aura.

Mother knew she could not change their decision. Dragokin are hardheaded beings. As stubborn as they are, even with inevitable death closing in, Dragokin are not easily frightened. Honor and pride flow heavily through our veins, as well as the hunger for battle and thirst for blood. Mother also knew for the Warriors to leave Father's side now would be to dishonor themselves underneath the heavens and in the eyes of their kin.

Father would do anything to ensure the safety of our kin, especially that of his love and own blood. Even at the cost of his position of Chief and his own life. The Chief of a clan is forbidden to stay in battle while the lives of innocents are still at risk. Father knew what he did was the only way to get Mother to leave while he stayed to fight.

*"Your Father's love has always been immense, **my Dragon**. From the very day our eyes met. From the battlefields we fought upon. From the very home we were ripped from,"* Mother said as we watched the Warriors prepare for close quarters combat, *"That very love will always remain with us, with you. Your heart will beat much like his and I am yet to realize if I must fear that or embrace it."*

With severe hesitation, Mother turned her eyes from the frontline. Her tears, her love, her very heart. She knew this was to be her last moments in the living world with Father. Her silence spoke a million words, and my heart heard every syllable.

Whilst gripping me tightly to her body, Mother began her own retreat towards the tree line in which our pack made trail. Her heart weighted heavily, breaking even more with every step. Her tear flow unstoppable. I placed my head where her heartbeat, and sensed the pain, the deep emotions that were maiming her spirit.

As we finally approached the masses of the innocent, I could see the tiresome looks on all their faces. It was as if their very lives were already draining from their bodies. Tired and weak, but still hopeful. The emotions I could feel were dense. Some giving up, some looking for light within the clouds.

Mother informed the pack of her new position as Chief. They were startled at first, but I could sense they were not surprised. She was one of the strongest Dragokin next to Father. Their undeniable strengths were their own. This is why our pack still believed there to be new hope. Mother ordered everyone to continue retreating away from the impending danger. That no matter what they hear, not to look back.

Before continuing, Mother stopped dead in her tracks. She turned back once more before we were completely out of sight. It was then and there that we witnessed the dwarves storming over the hills. An army much larger than what Father was leading.

The opposing force was certainly the same army that claimed many lives of our kin. The same army that forced us from our homelands. The same army that was beginning to seem to be an unstoppable force. An inevitable end.

Father was quick to engage them in a gruesome battle with all the Warriors from our pack. Our Warriors charged these foes with deadly intentions. Battle cries filled the air just before the clashing of steel. There was an endless spectrum of auras pushing violently against our foe's vile dark green aura.

Mother could not stand by any longer. She quickly turned in retreat. This moment would now be my last time laying eyes upon Father. But before completely disappearing into the forest, I glanced back to find Father within the crowd, only to truly witness Fathers unmatchable strengths.

Father was so effortlessly cutting through what seemed to be an endless wall of dwarves. I watched as he heaved his blade, as if it were a wooden training sword like he has trained me with before. Yet, his blade was a magnificent chunk of vicious steel. Such a savage weapon forced the blood of our enemies to endlessly spout from the necks and chests of those he sliced open.

Just before we vanished from sight, it was as if I felt familiar eyes upon me. I felt a love so immense that my own heart became filled with fire. There was this unknown feeling filling my soul, and then,

"**Forever, my Dragon shall soar**!" filled my ears. That voice, without mistake, was Father's.

CHAPTER ELEVEN
ONCE HUNTERS, NOW HUNTED

The sound of fallen branches snapping underneath tiresome feet. Blood, sweat, and tears mixed with the puddles of mud along our trail. I watched steam clouds rise above the exhausted crowd ahead of me as they panted. These were now the sounds that trailed within the whispering winds. It was the sound of what could be our last retreat.

Unfittingly, a gentle breeze brushed through the trees as we were making our desperate escape. I glanced at my surroundings while in Mother's arms, only to witness the tiresome faces all around. They were only becoming more breathless with every gaining step. This journey that had been endured, was surely taking its continued toll on our hearts and souls.

Fear hung around amongst us, heavy like sopping garments after a rain. Fear of losing everything and everyone. Fear of our stories, our traditions, our clan becoming nothing but faded memories. Victims to an enemy that we had never faced until now. A trail covered in cruel death and immense destruction.

Even at such a young age, I witnessed the honor and glory my kin was bestowed. The respect and love which I witnessed towards our people could never be forgotten. Those who visited our homelands proved this to be true. Now, our well respected and honored tribe had become trampled over. Trampled over with the boots of foes without honor in their hearts, minds, or souls.

I sensed immense fear in most of my kin, hope in others. Hatred towards our enemies in the rest. Even being war torn, Dragokin do not stand idle to be claimed by the heavens. No matter Warrior, Scholar, or common folk. Everything must be honored and faced with pride, even death itself.

Mother would always say,
"Our fate lies within our own hands. So long as we grip life tightly, we may control the reigns of even life itself."

These words would forever remain within my minds reach. Even now, her grip around me proved such words to be true. That no matter the road we have faced thus far, she had yet to release control of the reigns. She chose the fate ahead.

In the distance, the sound of Dragokin war horns echoed through this forest. One by one, these horns were becoming silenced. Mother's ears twitched to such a noise. Her heartbeat now becoming unsteady. Fluttering at the thought that we may yet still see Father live.

Mother stopped momentarily. The Dragokin from our pack continued retreating. All around, eyes set their glance on Mother's still position. None followed her actions. There was but one within the retreating crowds to find herself by Mother's side.

"*No matter what is to be heard, **we mustn't falter**!*" Artana said to Mother as Artana gripped her arm.

"*This is something I must face, something I must witness with my own gaze, Artana.* **Please, continue**. *Set our people on the righteous path as I would. I will soon to be at your heels,*" Mother whispered through trembling lips.

"*Yes...... **my Chief**,*" Artana replied before dashing forward to regain position with our pack.

Tears filled Mothers eyes as she feared for the worst. Her grip around me tightened. In the distance, there was silence that fell upon where the battle commenced. The air stiller than Mother's stance. Mother's heart was aching, I knew so because I felt such in this moment through my own heart.

We could not see the field in which the battle commenced. We could no longer even sense the energies of the Warriors from our pack. Only pain. Even worse, death. It was the ear shattering battle cry that made Mother flinch. A painful battle cry that sounded much like Father.

"HENGTUIN, KALASAG ANG MGA DRAGONS NG PROPESIYA, BIGYAN MO AKO NG AKING DRAGON'S WRATH!"

"HENGTUIN, SHIELD THE DRAGONS OF PROPHECY, GIVE ME MY DRAGON'S WRATH!"

Soon after, a thunderous crash shook the ground. A dark red and gray mist burst through the trees towards us. This energy, this power, it was beyond familiar. As the warm mist wrapped around us, it felt of Fathers touch. As this magical mist met our flesh, the aroma hinted of Father. The very energies seeping around us, that familiar to Father's soul.

I looked to Mother, and within her eyes I could sense she was aware of what happened. The pain I sensed within her was immense. As if her entire heart just shattered. Tears were flooding heavily from her eyes. Again, there was a gray aura illuminating her endless tears.

Mother's words quavered in the ancient Draconic language,

"Hanggang sa magkita tayo sa ulap, Mahal Kita, my Love..."
"Until we meet in the cloud, I love you, my Love."

In that moment it was as if time stood still. Mother's broken heart, the endless stream of silver illuminated tears, the red and gray mist settling. Mother was seeking clarity to these final chapters within our lives. To be one as a family once more. Together.

Before Mother could turn from the direction of the battlefield, quick approaching footsteps drew her attention. Mother's posture tensed and then she was consumed in her brilliant gray aura. This stance, this power, Mother harnessed energies so hastily that even my eyes may have missed it.

Red sparks illuminated within her aura. Like fierce lightning bolts from a heavy storm, these red sparks within her covered Mother's arms. Then, an immaculate and luminescent great sword formed within her hand. Emerging from the very glow was a monstrous fang. A faint screech howled through the winds as this weapon finished taking shape. The magical blade looked prehistoric, savage through and through.

Mother was focusing her attention, trying to reveal that in which was approaching through the mist. Her posture steadfast, blood flowing hastily. She wielded this ancient great sword with ease. She was readily armed for who, or what was to come through this mist. There was little to no magical energies to be sensed.

The footsteps were only getting louder. Although, this was not the sound of a retreating army. One individual was now becoming clear through the mist. It was Draxfur, from the Scouting masses. The Scouting masses which were not to be found through the fog. The look upon Mother's face was confused upon his reveal.

What remained of his traditional Scout's armor, was bloodied, and torn. Wounds covered his body; blood was spouting from his injuries. The fear on his face was all that was needed to express the coming situation. Such an expressed fear, that unlike any Dragokin has ever displayed. Such a fear, burning worry within Mother's heart, mind, and soulful being.

"M'Lady! You must continue pushing forward!" Draxfur shouted towards us in the distance.

Mother dropped her defensive stance, postured her body offensively, and wielded the mystical blade just a bit tighter. As she gripped me firmly against her body, she began to pace forwards towards Draxfur. Then, Mother noticed Draxfur was not alone. There were not familiar energies approaching fiercely through his trail, either.

As Draxfur was drawing his distance from the mist, he would violently volley arrows behind him. Not one, not two, but many arrows at a time. This was unlike an archer, there was no precision in his shots. We noticed that these arrows yielded their own auras, that there were magical energies bursting from within them.

Mother stopped when she noticed this. She knew that no matter the outcome of a battle, Dragokin would not risk the lives of their brethren with such reckless actions. That if there were truly more familiars behind him, he would not volley arrows so blindly. This made Mother grow even more worrisome.

"**M'LADY, YOU MUST RETREAT!**" Draxfur shouted once more.

Before Draxfur could reach us, an enormous Xenobeast lunged through the mist behind him. Taking Draxfur to the ground with his shoulder, tearing at the grips of the Xenobeasts garnet-stained teeth. Blood was spouting from his injury like a fountain. Mother screamed and started rushing towards Draxfur.

The Xenobeast moved as swift as a centipede, its six legs moving in a way that gave it the appearance of slithering. Its reptilian scales glinted and reflected the moonlight. Through the fog, the magical lights emitting from Draxfur's arrows shined within eyes darker than a midnight sky absent of moonlight. Trees crumbled within their paths; it was certain these creatures were built with nothing but muscle underneath armored shells. Lastly, within the explosion of their careless paths, was the clattering of razor-edged teeth serrating the insides of their mouths.

Xenobeasts live up to their reputation as blood hungry creatures. They are commonly found with Dwarves, such as the Dwarves that have been viciously hunting us down. Stories tell of these beasts growing in comparison to the size of full-grown oxen. It is also known that these beasts are creations of Irmina herself, and that the Dwarves struck a deal with the witch in order to befriend these creatures.

"**NO M'LADY! RETREAT!**" Draxfur painfully shouted as his last dying wish, the Xenobeast now ripping into his flesh more severely.

More of these beasts slowly emerged from the mist. Their numbers were grand, stretching along the tree line for as far as my eyes could see. These beasts pushed no further than the lead of their charge. The beast that claimed Draxfur seemed to be the Alpha of their numbers.

The Xenobeast that was assumed was the Alpha, soon released Draxfur from its grips. His lifeless body, mangled and bloodied, dropped dead on the ground beneath the beast. This creature looked directly at us. The screeching roar that emerged from it shattered our ears.

Mother was still hesitant to retreat, even being outnumbered. I could feel her becoming tense, consumed in a rage. Her blood was flowing quickly, and heart pounded for war. Mother was bestowed the honor Shield Maiden because she was fierce. She had fought many battles at Father's side in the past.

Mother's rage was immense. This gray aura with fierce red sparks was now swirling around us violently. Slowly gripping to her body, this once vapor like substance was becoming an armored solid on her battle tattered being. She removed her grip from around me and it was like her very aura held me there against her chest.

Mother extended her arm which was sheltering me, and the red sparks began to cover it. Her aura seeped from her fingertips, and in midair, she began painting an ancient symbol. It was much like the ancient symbol I have seen within my recent dreams.

Soon after, the archaic symbol illuminated brightly and split the very fabric of Nydeli. A darkened portal opened and what seemed to be the hilt of a blade emerged.

Mother grabbed hold of this hilt and with her almighty strength, she ripped another mystical blade from this portal. This energy I felt, this power. It was beyond surreal. This mystical armor and weapons, breathtaking. To witness such power was certainly astonishing. Mother's eyes were beyond intense. Where her heart once beat, was now completely still, silent.

This newly formed armor Mother has bestowed looked as if it was shaped like a dragon. Her wings spread wide as this aura continued to form around her body. Thickened scales plated this armor's surface, and spikes protruded through.

Before Mother's face was covered by a dragon skull helm, I witnessed red streams within her silver eyes. Her very breath yielded red sparks. This was the rage of war that flowed within Dragokin blood. This was the fierce power that was caged within my kin. Dragokin were not a force to be reckoned with.

As she looked around to our enemies, her heart started to beat within her chest once again. This time the rhythm of her heart was racing uncontrollably. I could sense it was as if she were about to lose control of her very being, this rage within her was not to be tamed.

Mother's breathing patterns were heavy and yielded no steady rhythm. It was only when she looked down at my concerned eyes that her heart found a steady pace. The rage within her began calming, the blood within her, cooling. Although her heart was beating steadily now, there was still a weight heavily upon it.

In the distance, beyond the clattering of the Xenobeasts, we could faintly hear Draxfur's dying breath. The sound of blood gurgling, and the painful attempt at a muster for words. There were no words. None at all. Only the sounds of a dying man.

The weight of Draxfur's death on Mother's heart only burdened her more. She knew Draxfur's fate had been met. This was something I could sense she did not want to accept. We had lost so much. Even Father's life had been taken. That no matter the efforts made, this seemed to be a lost battle, a forfeited war.

This was not a battle she must face, especially not alone. With the utmost hesitation, Mother dropped her battle stance. Her armor slowly began to crack. Pieces fell from the primeval armor, only to return to the vapor that it once was.

"*Please, forgive me!*" were Mother's silent and broken words.

The ancient swords Mother was wielding, they illuminated brightly before dispersing as well. Mother's grip found me once again. She pressed me tightly against her body. Her gray illuminated tears were rolling down her cheeks and coating my flesh. If there was any love or life within her heart, it was surely difficult to sense. Underneath Mothers breath she whispered:

"**Hengtuin, Gabayan Mo Kami**!"
"*Hengtuin, Guide Us!*"

As Mother spoke those words in the ancient tongue of Dragons, it was as if her very breath, her words, were sparked with flames. Mother looked up towards the Xenobeasts. The creature that took Draxfur to the ground was holding its position above Draxfur's lifeless body.

Slowly, Mother was now positioning herself for retreat. The energy which once was the armor and weapons were absorbing into Mother's being. Her eyes locked onto the lead creature, feet slowing positioning to pounce in the opposite direction.

The Xenobeast leading the enemies charge was fierce. There was this look upon it that gave me the feeling this beast had witnessed many wars itself. Dead in the eyes, scales riddled with scars. The fierce beast paced forward, slowly. Then, with not a moment to spare, the beast released a screeching rattle that enraged the others.

It was as if there were wooden chimes clattering in fierce winds. Much like the rattle of a snake when approached with hostility. These beasts were in an absolute frenzy, scratching for the command. Once the clattering of these beasts halted, the lead beast burst with another screech. This time, the endless line of Xenobeasts began to charge. It was more than likely the Dwarves spotted us retreating into the forest, that they ordered their Xenobeasts to hunt us while they engaged our kin in gruesome battle.

Mother knew this was her moment to break stance. With no time to spare, Mother turned to continue our retreat. The aura that was around us was fully consumed within Mother's being. She used that energy to dash in the direction away from our enemies. Such speed sent the ground shaking beneath us and left our enemies in the dust.

Xenobeasts were created through dark magic for but one reason, to kill. Desperate times fell upon the witch Irmina. Her last effort to remind the world of her existence, was to create blood hungry beasts that would forever spill blood in her name. To reign death over Nydeli for what wrongs she felt were done to her. The witch has been long gone, but her blood thirsty creatures still breathe.

As Mother was dashing forward to be one with our pack, the Xenobeasts followed. The Xenobeasts were not nearly as fast as Mother, however they did in fact yield great speed. Trampling through the forest behind us, nothing was slowing them down. Only destruction, chaos, and death followed their trail.

"We must warn the others within our pack, my Dragon. For these beasts are relentless and surely do not fatigue like us." Mother worried as she continued pushing her body, heart, and mind beyond their critical conditions.

It was not too long before we found ourselves back within the trail of our pack. I could smell the blood, sweat, and tears. I could hear the tiresome panting of everyone's efforts to escape. The vegetation around proved heavy numbers pushing through this forest.

In the distance we witnessed stragglers from the crowds of our kin, that there were some stopping in hopes to catch breath. Tending to injuries that have been suffered. Those bearing more strength within them were attempting to help those on their last breath.

Upon the sight of Mother's return, there was rejoice. That was, until they witnessed the look upon Mother's face, the devastation within her eyes, **"WE MUST MOVE! DRAGON'S FURY!"** Mother shouted as she leaped in the air, spinning, and barraging hundreds of magical orbs behind her.

The sounds of the Xenobeasts charge was beginning to grow louder, now mixing with the wisping of Mother's violent spells. With Mother's speed we were able to make some distance between, but not enough to break these creatures from our trail. As these orbs of magical energies were splashing behind us, bursting with destruction, the trees fell within the distance behind us. Loud screeching emerged through the smoke and fire, the Xenobeasts were soon to become visible.

I had never witnessed Dragokin move so fast before on foot. Breaking from the still position we found these Dragokin in, they were using the full length of their stride, maneuvering through the harsh conditions of the forest. We were making haste through the trees, but the prodigious Xenobeasts were not far behind us.

"Do not give in now! With our enemy at our heels, we must push forward!" Mother shouted as we finally regained position with the masses of our pack.

Mother held me tightly in her arms, but I was still able to see behind us. It was not long before I began to witness continued bloodshed. Mother did not speak false words, these beasts that hunted us yielded no signs of fatigue. Their eyes were piercing, even from a distance. Such eyes only craved death.

I witnessed the Xenobeasts viciously taking down Dragokin from my pack one by one. They first tackled to the ground the already injured or sick because they were the easiest of prey, most of which were the stragglers we first found. The ones that breathed little to no life.

The Xenobeasts were turning my kin into puddles of flesh and blood. Quickly dashing forward to the next Dragokin within their reach. It was as if they were only maiming our people, to prevent any chance of retreat. The Dragokin that were being hunted sounded heartbreaking battle cries as they were taken to the ground.

Some of the Dragokin amongst us were the elderly who had faced their days on the battlefield. Decrepit and crippled from many battles of the past. Most lived as scholars to the younger Warriors, only to teach of battle through books. Their bodies were not built for war anymore, but their minds still yielded the flames for battle.

I could sense they knew their time in this world would meet its end. I could also sense pride within their hearts. To return to the battlefield once more, even at the cost of their unavoidable death. To protect the ones they loved, to stand for those who are unable to stand for themselves. To greet this enemy at our heels with an unbreakable, beating Dragokin heart.

One elderly Dragokin shouted, **"Though I have not been a Warrior in many ages, it will be an honor to shed the blood of our enemies, even knowing I will draw my last breath on this day!"** and then stopped dead in his tracks, conjuring what magical energies he could.

Another Dragokin shouted, **"MY CHIEF! FOR HONOR AND GLORY!"** and was soon to also stop dead in his tracks.

Others joined them with their own last words. Praising their loved ones, apologizing that their fate would be met. Shouting to the heavens and demanding a cold glass of spirits when Hengtuin guides them under his wings. Most of the elderly did not wield blades, but the magical energies that emitted from their bodies were vast. It was as if they were using their very life force to greet the enemy in battle.

Magnificent auras of many shades began to illuminate from those who faced our enemies. Magical weapons appeared from thin air. Fireballs, ice shards, and lightning bolts projected from the hands of others. Trees became full of life and were attacking those of their controller's commands. Shadows of the Xenobeasts were betraying their owners and pulling them into the darkness. The elders who stood and fought were surely falling to our enemy, but they took a stand to protect those still virgins to battlefields.

Upon gaining distance from our enemies, Mother stopped for a moment. Her tears had yet to halt. Her heart only continued to break. Underneath her breath she spoke, *"May Hengtuin guide those on the battlefield, and honor your sacrifice!"*

Even with the efforts of the elders, the Xenobeasts were ripping them apart, stripping what life they yet yielded. They were taking them from Nydeli so effortlessly. It was as if there were no fear or regret within the hearts of those who stood and fought. Even as the gruesome scene unfolded all around them, I watched in awe as my kin stood broad shouldered and stone faced. They were fearless. Their fate was chosen by their own decisions, not the heavens. The elders made a brave sacrifice, however it only temporarily set back the Xenobeasts.

The once legendary Warriors fell one by one. Too old for more powerful magic or to wield a blade properly. I witnessed these Warriors cut down the Xenobeasts in numbers, but our enemies seemed endless.

"The names of these Warriors will never be forgotten. If any of our kin are to survive, they will remember those who made the ultimate sacrifice. Songs will be sung through spirit halls of their honor, of their sacrifice, of their bravery!" Mother finished before following the remaining numbers of the retreat.

Once the Xenobeasts finished off the elders who stood and fought, they continued their hunt. There were younger Dragolings within our numbers, those who were not being carried like myself. Their shorter legs prevented them from achieving greater strides.

Unfortunately, these Dragolings were falling behind the rest of us. Some of the remaining elders turned in attempts to save them, but by then it was far too late. Their cries for help pierced our ears. They were left to be torn to pieces by the savage Xenobeasts.

I was not scared or shaken by the situation. I was mostly curious.

Why were we chased from our home?

Why were such vicious actions being taken against my kin?

It was as if the emotions I should yield only burdened my mind with questions.

During that stage of my life, I could only vaguely understand the words of my fellow Dragokin. I could only sense their emotions. So, I just observed everything going on around me. I questioned why I was not feeling the fear, pain, or heartbreak that the others were expressing.

As I looked to the remaining Dragokin running from these blood driven beasts, I noticed those that remained also held onto young ones with dear life, much like Mother was holding onto me. Some had but one, some struggled with many young ones.

There were but two Dragokin that pulled my attention. One of them with silver scales that reflected a spectrum of colors when the light met them, her eyes ebbed with the same dance of hues, speckling like an opal. Such beautiful colors flowed through her eyes, as a gentle stream does during a subtle season of spring. Her wings reflected the same striking qualities. As though they were transparent and only yielded iridescent traits.

The other female, Artana, had immaculate gold scales. It was as if she was showered in the purest of gold from Nydeli and sprinkled in diamonds. In contrast, her eyes were fierce. Crimson red, like fresh blood, with streaks of gold flowing through them. Her wings seemed to be armored, but still she was quick on her feet.

They both seemed to be around Mother's age. They too were holding onto hatchlings with dear life. The hatchlings within their arms portrayed more than just similar traits to those who carried them. I could only wonder as to why out of the many, these were the ones my eyes attracted towards.

Upon my gaze, Artana was soon to greet my glance with her own. She was quick to approach Mother while we continued to make a desperate escape from our enemies. I still remember the fearful yet strong tone in her voice,

"**Take Norixius with you and I will buy you time, Sister**," her lips trembled while handing Mother the hatchling that she was protecting, "**If we are to live on, it will be through them**," Artana continued calmly to Mother with tears in her eyes.
"*Artana, No!* **You cannot expect me to allow this!**" Mother cried out with her own heartbroken voice.

"**No, I do not expect you to allow me to do this**. *I expect you to give me hope that our children will see a future*! Though knowing my dragon will grow into this world without me in it, **I would rather die than allow our enemies to claim him!**" Artana admitted, tears flowing deeply from her eyes.

Mother began to argue with her as she did with my Father, "**NO! Time has proven that there is always another way! That we mustn't always believe sacrifice is the only answer!**"

I began to sense a calming within Artana's spirit and heart. It seemed as if she did not hear Mother's words, or she did but chose not to entertain Mother with discussion. Her decision has already been set in stone, "**There is no time for argument little sister**! I have stood by your decisions for what feels like forever, ***this my dear sister****, will be the last time I am to be able to protect you. To protect them*," Artana said with such love emitting from her heart.

I lost focus on the tense words they were exchanging. I was too focused on this hatchling whom Mother was now carrying in her other arm. He was different than I. His eyes were deeply golden with streams of crimson red flowing through them. Opposite of Artana's own eyes. His wings were not only bones like mine, they appeared metallic with only a shimmer of gold.

I could sense he was in fear from the situation. His eyes were teary and his heart, shaken. He held his face close to Mother's shoulder, covering his ears with both hands. He was shaking uncontrollably within Mother's arms. I for some reason, did not share those same feelings. I could only assume that this golden eyed Dragoling may have been on Nydeli longer than myself. Maybe that his understanding of the world manifested faster than my own. That he was more aware of what was truly unfolding on this journey.

I could not understand why I felt so fearless. I was young, this was true, but trying to understand everything was out of my comprehension. By this stage in my life, I had never witnessed such vast counts of death or fearsome battle. Yet, my emotions were not matched to those around.

The hatchling within Mother's grip with me was soon to attempt to lunge out of Mother's arms. She gripped him tightly as he reached his arms out behind Mother. His little legs kicking at her, hoping that her grip would break. He cried out desperately while his eyes filled with tears.

As I returned my own focus to our surroundings, I noticed that Artana was not running next to us anymore. I took a glance behind us only to notice she stopped dead in her tracks. Next to her stood what seemed to remain of the Shield Maidens that Artana was always found around. What magical energies remained in their bodies was surely about to be dispersed amongst the battlefield in a last standing effort of survival.

Their bodies became consumed with many different colors. Artana's aura glowed a magnificent yellow. Other Shield Maidens were glowing a deep ocean blue. A small majority of them glowed as green as the forest itself. Mystical weapons were being conjured from thin air. Those same weapons found their rightful place within those Dragokin's hands.

The golden eyed hatchling continued to struggle within Mother's arms. He was now scratching and biting at Mother, but she held him tight as we continued retreating. Tears were now gushing from his own eyes while desperately roaring for his Mother. This was truly the day that I could feel my Mother's own heart fading from this world.

Artana's tear-filled eyes connected with mine as we were drawing our distance. She had a smile on her face despite the situation. She waved a kiss towards the golden eyed hatchling. Her focus then returned towards the imminent danger. She wielded in her hands a golden spear. The spear looked as if it were spiked with the teeth of a dragon.

Artana and those with her were the last stand. The last fighting force from my clan, my kin. Thousands had fallen along this trail of reckoning. First our Warriors. Next our elders and children. Lastly, all of the remaining Shield Maidens were forming to be the last defensive line in our retreat. There was only a handful of us left.

Before we drew our distance too far, I witnessed a Xenobeast lunge towards Artana. She fiercely drove her spear into its chest and suddenly it burst into a golden mist. One by one the last fighting force of my pack were falling but taking with them as many beasts as they could. Artana was holding strong. Leaping from one Xenobeast to the next. She was quite the glorious Warrior.

The others who stood with Artana noticed her fierce stance. Their own fires inside suddenly became sparked by witnessing such a beating heart like Artana's. They were stripping life from as many Xenobeasts that their remaining energies and abilities allowed, fighting with their very lives on the line.

This fire did not burn much longer. The last moment I remember of Artana, a Xenobeast had lunged towards her and wrapped its jaws around her neck. It took her to the ground, with blood spewing from her injuries. There was no cry out in pain from Artana. She was soon to grip her immaculate spear which was almost buried in the dirt beside her. She then threw her mighty spear powerfully towards the heavens. There was a brilliant gold aura that trailed within the spears path. As it finally met the clouds, the skies glimmered momentarily before returning to normal.

Artana's last words began to shower over us,

"Hengtuin, Panatilihin ang iyong apoy sa loob ng mas nakababatang Dragons. DRAGONS WRATH!"
"Hengtuin, Keep your fire inside the younger Dragons. DRAGONS WRATH!"

Mother's eyes were soon to widen upon hearing such words. She did not halt her retreat. Quite the opposite, Mother pushed herself even harder in attempts to gain more distance while her tears lit our path. Mother began to rush even faster, gripping us more tightly and exhausting more of her strength with every step.

The air throughout the forest began to whirl around in a violent manner. The very fabric of Nydeli was beginning to morph around us. Nearby rocks seemed to begin to morph into gold. After completion, they would burst into a gold mist and gravitate towards Artana's location.

Mother leaped fiercely into the air in attempts to take flight above the trees. She failed to achieve a powerful enough thrust to become air bound multiple times. She did not quit. One attempt after another. She continued to push her body beyond its own limits. I noticed a few others attempting to take flight as well. This was not an easy task to achieve. Given the situation and our surroundings, it would take everything left in them to take flight. After all we had been through, I knew it took immense strength to take flight with little to no life within one's body and mind.

Opportunity presented itself within Mother's path. Others noticed this and began trailing her. Mother found a fallen tree and began to run along its path. Upon reaching the end, she gave all that she had left in her for one final leap and a violent thrust with her wings.

Mother was fighting to ascend out of deadly reach, a battle cry that sounded much like Artana filled the air. The golden eyed hatchling was more familiar to this voice. Giving all that he had beyond his tears, he let out his own ear shattering cry.

I peered over Mother's shoulder again, I noticed it was too late for those too tiresome in the remainder of my pack. Xenobeasts were already at our heels. They took down all the those who could not take flight, even some who were able to but could not achieve such a distance considered safe from the Xenobeasts. I could hear the horror being unleashed underneath the trees below us as we were finally able to ascend the skies.

Those who were able to escape and take flight scattered in all different directions. I could only assume that with such dire numbers this was the best option. To spread out and disband. What used to be a vast and powerful Dragokin pack was now diminished. Only few had survived.

The forest was filled with the dying cries from the Dragokin in our pack. Mother's eyes were yet to dry from heavy tears. The golden eyed hatchling also continued shedding tears. I could only press my head against Mother's chest and close my own eyes. To sense the feelings that burdened their hearts.

The cries for help eventually became noiseless. As we flew further away, we found cover within the darkness of the skies. The chaos that waged around us, now silent. The odor of death that stenched our nostrils, now scentless. The horrors stained within our eyes, now only reflected the darkening skies above.

CHAPTER TWELVE
MOTHER'S TEARS

I was beginning to grow restless. Everything I had witnessed so far forced my mind to be rattled, heart to be shaken. My eyes feared shutting at the thought of losing sight of Mother's luminous gaze. Pools of tears still formed within them, as if they were brilliant, polished ores resting in a clear rivers water.

My head upon her chest, proved to find her own worrisome heart. My arms wrapped tightly around her warm embrace. Whilst the golden eyed hatchling wearingly slept in her other arm, I could only assume exhaustion from the devastation within his heart had finally overcome him.

I had no concept of time. I watched as the sun rose through the distant clouds. I observed as the sun stretched across the skies. Then finally, I witnessed the sun fall beyond the great horizon. It was becoming dark, and soon the sun's brother would greet us with night skies.

Through everything tragically experienced, I looked forward to watching the skies. The most beautiful sight to bear witness, when the sun and moon both meet their respective horizons. Variegated shades of orange streaking through one horizon. A calm dark blue consuming the opposite. It was a solace that I looked forward to in some of those dark moments.

Everything that had happened, everything I had witnessed thus far, was now starting to flash before my eyes. Father's last battle cry. Draxfur's last dying breath. Artana's last shout to be heard by the heavens. All the final cries from kin within my pack, were now ringing through my head.

As the night's sky began to gloom over, Nydeli's slight zephyr whirled around us. The now soundless air only filled with trembling sorrow which seeped from Mother. Her tears continued to fall as we soared high above. The moonlight meeting her tears resembled that much similar to gentle raindrops.

Mother continued to draw our distance further away from our enemies. As I continued to listen to Mother's heart, I could sense she was becoming even more tiresome. I could feel that she was using everything within her to stay high above the forest floor. Her wings were beginning to flutter with less strength and eventually she spread them wide to just soar above the trees.

*"Everything mustn't be lost or forfeited young dragons! With my very heart, soul, and being, I will see to it that your lives will continue. **That you may breathe life and become the dragons you are destined to be!**"* Mother whispered as she gripped us tightly against her chest.

So, there we were, soaring above lands that our kin have been slaughtered upon. Mother's mind did not once find ease. Her eyes constantly scanning the surface below. Ears twitching, listening beyond what was commonly heard. I could feel the worry within her heart through my own. Mother only continued to grow more breathless.

We had been gliding over the trees for quite some time. Mother's strength was keeping our shadows casted below, yet her flight patterns would falter from time to time, and she would stagger. We were feeling as if we were to never set foot upon Nydeli's surface again. An endless plateau of trees below us. Suddenly, there was a distinct sound that caught Mother's attention.

Within the nights silence, our ears were pulled towards a relieving sound. Far from the ocean, but water yet rippled nearby. Through the darkness Mother surveyed Nydeli's surface. It was only then that she noticed, through the moonlight, that the trees of the forest were split by Nydeli's forces of nature. There was a river nearby.

The moon had stretched quite the distance through the skies. From the point in which we were, it dwindled directly above our heads. This proved us to be a vast distance from the bloodshed. Mother was still so cautious, but she slowly glided towards the rivers serenading tides. As we descended from the skies, Mother gathered what magical energies were left within her.

Her eyes began to shine brightly, her body consumed in this subtle gray aura. She spun her head around, eyes witnessing all that was around us. As she did this, the worry within her heart was not pounding much like before. It was as if she knew there was nothing to worry about here and now. That we may in fact be beyond our enemy's sights.

We soon discovered the river through the trees. An opening, an opportunity for Mother to land without worry of the complete unknown. Without worry of a blind landing within such hostile lands. I could feel this restored hope within Mother's heart, that opportunity yet presents itself.

Mother shifted her flight pattern to follow the river's tides downstream. Our eyes finally bore witness to solid, open grounds surrounding the glistening rivers waters. There was relief showering over Mother. Once she finished surveying what was to come ahead, she slowly began to lower her flight pattern.

Attempting to keep control of herself, I could feel her continued strenuous stagger. Her eyes were scanning every detail below us. Her ears listening beyond what could be seen and felt. Her trust of the world itself was now a sliver within her heart. As if she felt Nydeli has betrayed her, that there was nothing good beneath the skies.

I felt Mother's grip tightening around me. Such a grip woke the golden eyed hatchling from his own tiring slumber. We both wrapped our arms tightly around Mother. Her own grip around us proved that she was bracing us for landing, that her own exhaustion and worrisome heart was not prepared to land properly.

As we neared the forest floor, Mother secured us in her arms more so. She then wrapped her wings around us. Doing so forced Mother to lose absolute control of her flight path. She knew her wings would be providing us with greater protection.

Through Mother's luminescent wings, the surface was becoming visibly closer. I looked deeply into her beautiful shining eyes as we fell. Mother just smiled as we harshly plummeted into Nydeli's surface. There was now pain within Mother's eyes. We continued to crash upon the sharpened rocks and hardened grounds beneath, but still Mother was able to protect us from any harm.

It was quite the violent landing, considering Mother's own weakening condition. It was as if I could hear her flesh ripping and tearing, her bones breaking and snapping. Mother's eyes had shut through the landing. As if she did not want us to witness her pain.

We were soon to reach a violent halt, as Mother's body was slammed against a boulder along the river's edge. Her eyes widened, and she displayed a face in severe pain. She could not help but to shout as this pain became inflicted upon her. My own heart began to worry after witnessing this.

I could not even imagine the agony Mother was suffering. The immense pain not only within her mind, but her heart, and upon her flesh. The deeply inflicted gashes upon her very soul. Shield Maiden. Chief. She was a Queen within my eyes and heart. Our enemies believed they have reduced such a powerful soul to a mere captive, only delaying the captures chains.

We had witnessed firsthand it truly is not chaining our foes wish to bind us within. It is agonizing death itself. They wish to strip our very breath. To take our names and have them be lost within the sands of time. To bloody our history and shred the tomes in which bind our existence to the living plane.

So, Mother's true pain finally burst through the impenetrable shell that was her very being. Through it all, through what we have suffered, Mother had yet to display true agony. Until now. Now it seemed the weight upon us was too heavy to bear. Mother had endured so much anguish by this point. Her heart completely shattered. Soul ripped apart. It was as if no amount of suffering would injure Mother more than what had already been done, that our journey has truly became a scar that will forever burden her heart, mind, and soul.

Through her heartbroken eyes, Mother glanced deeply within my own. Mother slowly unwrapped her wings from around us. Their luminescent glow flickering, the nights ghostly shadows were now consuming their light. Her grip began to loosen, and soon her arms fell to her sides. Mother's eyes lost their luminosity. Her aura began to vanish. Mother's breath was beginning to find a worrisome pace. A pace that I have only heard within the last moments of one's life.

I placed my little hands upon Mother's tear-soaked cheek. My fingertips tracing the trails in which have been dried and soaked again. The golden eyed hatching rolled off from Mother's chest. I just sat there, staring at Mother with utmost concern. Attempting to keep my hold upon Mother for as long as I could.

"My dragons, I have failed. I have failed your Fathers. I have failed your Mother. I have failed our people." Mother mustered through the blood and tears of her being.

    The Golden Eyed Hatchling curled himself into a ball. He was tucking his wings around him and crying within his own solitude. I did not leave Mother's side. I noticed a vast amount of blood against the boulder Mother had slammed against. Pools of Mother's blood was now forming around us.
    To realize this fate, this devastation, might truly be unavoidable. My heart began to rattle, Mother took notice of such. Mother placed her hands upon mine, again glanced deeply into my eyes, and exposed her beautiful smile. A smile that warmed even the sun and stars themselves.
    I was quick to grab hold of Mothers arm. I hugged it tightly with my own tears finding their home within my eyes. It was not long before I too whimpered. The realization that this was the end, that all the lives of my kin have been claimed. This is when my heart finally accepted the toll in which had been paid.
    Mother's hand slowly wiped my hair from my eyes. Her warm palm was soon to soak up my tears. Mother lifted my chin in such a way that my eyes could meet hers. With her own tear-filled eyes Mother whispered,

"*I knew it would not be long before I witnessed your Father's strength break within you my Dragon, and now that of your Mother's heart shows within your eyes.*"

Mother was now using what little life that remained within her. The amount of blood that Mother has lost, the ever-growing pool, now streaming towards the river. Mother was beginning to show fatal traits. Yet, she continued to use what strength she had left. Mother continued to live, ignoring the obvious signs of looming demise.

Mother pulled me close to her heart. She wrapped her arms around me and whispered, *"Your heart will forever beat with two rhythms my Dragon. War and Strength like your Father's, Love and Balance like mine. Forever follow these rhythms my Dragon. Forever follow your heart!"*

I sensed Mother knew this would be her last embrace with me in her arms. She cherished this moment and was savoring every bit of it. With utmost hesitation, Mother released me from her warm embrace. Mother then said, *"With what is left beating within me, I will see to it that you, young ones, become a distant thought within the minds who hunt us."*

The world still yielded warmth from Nydeli's sunlight. Yet, the moons ghostly shadow spared not a moment to infiltrate the warmth around. The river's mellow tides reflected the moon's light. As the river flowed, this light gamboled around the river's edges. Our shadows were dancing within the night.

Mother slid me from off her chest. She slowly rolled herself from her back and soon pushed herself from Nydeli's surface. Mother began to crawl towards the river. The rocks beneath were freshly stained with Mother's blood. The subtle darkness revealed a trail, a trail of blood that shimmered from the point in which we first landed.

There were many sharp rocks that covered the river's edges. All in which were now drenched in blood. My eyes pierced over to Mother, only to witness severe gashes upon her flesh. Violently, her blood leaked from these gruesome injuries. Mother fell to her chest as she reached the rivers flowing stream.

I began to crawl hastily towards her with concern. I was cutting my own legs in the process. Nothing severe as Mother's injuries though. Mother heard me making my way towards her. Her head turned towards me to reveal that her eyes not only filled with tears still but were also gleaming flawless shades of her gray aura.

The Golden Eyed Hatchling broke himself from his shell, only upon hearing our own movement. He attempted to find his ground. Falling after a few steps but continuing towards us. Mother could not help but to chuckle at the sight of this, her blood now dripping from her lips.

Mother began taking handfuls of mud from the riverbank and mixed it all within a puddle. As we found ourselves by Mothers side, she reached out to pull us in closer to her. Even through all we had suffered, Mother had a delicate smile on her face. It was as if she did not want me to become concerned for her again.

Mother was coating the Golden Eye Hatchling and myself with the mud she was gathering. Leaving no flesh uncovered. She did not coat herself in the process. Mother was acting as if whatever were to come, she would not be along that trail.

So, I began to gather little handfuls of mud. I began spreading the bits of mud I gathered across Mother. She looked to me as I was doing this and smiled through her tears. Mother continued watching as I was gathering more mud to place upon her own flesh. Soon, her hand met mine and freed my hands of the thickened mud.

"Need not worry for me, my Dragon." Mother chuckled while wiping the oozing mud from my eyes, *"I need you two Dragons to stay put, but only for a moment."*

Afterwards, Mother was struggling to find her ground. She pushed through her pain to find herself to her feet. Slowly, Mother limped towards the nearby tree line. Even through the pain, Mother was moving with purpose. As if there were not seemingly fatal injuries decorating her body.

The Golden Eyed Hatchling and I sat by the river, and we witnessed Mother gathering logs and fallen branches. Stacking them into nearby piles. Arranging them side by side. Then, Mother was ripping massive vines from the nearby trees. Once all was gathered that Mother needed, she kneeled next to her piles of resources.

Mother was arranging the logs and branches; she was using the vines to bind them together. Her hands yielded a subtle and flickering aura as she was crafting this object. Her eyes were now flickering as well. I knew her magical energies were diminishing because her heart was connected with mine. I knew within my own heart, that hers was hastily fading.

I could sense Mother was devastated from what was about to happen. Mother was the strongest Dragokin in my eyes. Other than Father, there were no others I have witnessed to match her strength in spirit and heart. However, I have never felt so much pain emerge from her heart. I had a feeling this was the last time I would hear Mother's nurturing voice.

"If you are to breathe life, young ones, I must lead our enemies away from you," she said while rushing to finish this object which was now appearing to be a raft of sorts, *"there is not much time, and I will not see my young ones fall to these beasts that hunt us. You will carry our love with you and* **one day become the Dragokin we wish for you to be.***"*

I could not completely understand her words or what was going on. Before I could even try to make sense of the situation, Mother was setting the completed raft along the rivers bed-halfway set within the river's tides. Its other half secured to the river's edge.

Thickened tears were forming in Mother's beautiful silver eyes as she approached us. Mother picked us up one at a time and set us on the raft whilst it was floating in the river. What remained of Mother's heart and soul was now vanishing from her being. Seeping from her core and waning with the breeze. Though her tears could prove otherwise, Mother held a stoic look upon her face.

Mother began to wrap vines around our wrists that secured us to the raft, *"My Dragons, use your minds to think of these vines as your Mother's grip. They will hold you close and keep you safe!"* Mother whispered as she finished securing us to the raft.

I was soon to notice magical energies bleeding from Nydeli's surface around Mother. Her hands then began to illuminate brightly, brighter than I had witnessed before, with her gray aura. The red sparks from before now sizzling within her flesh. All across Mother's body, mystical symbols formed with these red sparks and began to move towards her hands.

Mother placed her hands on both of my shoulders. My scales began to sear. Anyone within earshot could hear my shoulders sizzling underneath her palms. I flinched for a moment from the pain but was too focused on Mother's eyes. My heart to concerned for the pain in which Mother was suffering.

The feeling of love and heartbreak was battling within her like fierce dragons over plunder. Her very aura filtered towards her hands, soon filling my body and soul with what remained inside Mother. There were magical energies continuing to seep from Nydeli's surface, absorbing into Mother, and soaking into my shoulders.

Once Mother was finished with me, I sat there and observed as she did the same thing with the Golden Eyed Hatchling. He was squirming from the pain in which this inflicted, but Mother did not stop until she was completed. The Golden Eyed Hatchling continued to cry in pain even as Mother was finished.

Mother branded us with the very symbols that were on her body. The pain was truly immense. When she released her hands, a bright gray symbol was left upon our shoulders. Slowly other symbols began to cover our bodies just as it did with hers. Breathtaking auras surrounded us. Underneath Mother's breath I could hear the chant in the ancient Dragon's Tongue.

"Sa aking hininga, Sa aking puso, So aking kaluluwa,
(In my breath, in my heart, in my soul,)

Ibinibigay ko ang lahat na nasa dugo ng aking Dragon sa mga may simbolo,
(I give everything that is in the blood of my Dragon to those who have the symbol,)

Hengtuin, Gabayan ang kanilang landas at huminga ang purong buhay sa mga bulaklak na ito,
(Hengtuin, Guide their path and breathe the pure life into these flowers,)

Dahil sila ay Drago at dapat nilang sindihan ang kanilang makapangyarihang apoy!"
(Because they are Drago and they must light their powerful fires!)

    Mother chanted and the heavens themselves shook and roared. As Mother continued chanting these words, the pain became even more intense. The symbols on our bodies were now glowing different shades of the spectrum, and there was this mystical feeling that overwhelmed me.
    The clouds above began to form around, lightning filled the skies and once again it was as if Dragons themselves were soaring beyond them. Soon after, a massive beam of light pierced through Mother. These images of dragons were dispersing from her body, and directly into the clouds.

I should have been knocked unconscious instantly from the pain I have suffered, but I was fighting the urge to sleep. The golden eyed hatchling was not as strong. He fell unconscious instantly while I struggled to stay awake. I remember seeing tears flood from Mother's eyes as if they were the source of the river's flowing tide.

I reached towards Mother while crying for her warm touch. She looked down at me with her tear-filled eyes. Mother whispered something underneath her breath, and then she casted us down the river on the raft. As she did, Mother was shouting to the heavens above. I too was now roaring, reaching towards Mother, but the vines of the raft kept me bound to it.

Right before my eyes were slowly forced to close, I remember seeing Mother in an absolute rage. The rage I have only witnessed once before. Mother turned once more to look at us with her tear-soaked eyes.

"**DRAGON'S WRATH!**" Mother shouted, and then her body became consumed in a bright gray light. So bright that my eyes fell shut and I did not possess the strength to open them again.

That was the last time I saw my loving Mother in the living world.

"DRAGON'S WRATH!" echoed within the darkness.

"DRAGON'S WRATH!" continued to repeat within my mind.

"DRAGON'S WRATH!" shouted by voices unrecognizable to me.

"Waken, Young Drago!" silenced the chanting within this dark and empty void.

Once again, I was in this unknown yet becoming familiar place. It was the dark room in which my first dream happened. The candles lighting a path within this void. As the flames light danced around, ancient symbols began to illuminate upon the walls.

There was much more light now than before. Massive pillars protruded through the ground, decorated with skulls of many races, beings, and creatures. Where their eyes would be, soon lit up with different colors and shades of the pigment gamut. They were not eyes, physically, yet I felt such upon me.

I was not the older version of myself, nor merely an apparition, but my current self in flesh and blood. I could not help but to wonder if this was a dream, or the end to it all. With one hand in front of the other, I crawled in the direction that the candles were beginning to light. Slowly they revealed this archaic tomb in which I was now bound within.

"Follow my path, Young Drago. Follow your heart!" *the same voice from before called out.*

As I continued through this room, apparitions of Dragokin would rise between the pillars. Those that looked much like War Chiefs. Standing directly opposite of them, Shield Maidens who portrayed similar traits. Similar armor. Similar stances to those in which they stood across from.

My eyes were amazed from what I was witnessing while crawling through this room. This empty void which seemed to become filled with life with the spirits of others watching as I passed by. I stopped for a moment and shook my head, this felt beyond real. Too real to only be a dream.

I lost focus on how much path remained, as I was focusing on everything within this tomb, my eyes drew my mind ever so curious. It was as if these were the halls of the heavens, yet there was no grand feast. The lingering spirits of these Dragokin were unfamiliar. They only stood, watching as I crawled past.

"There, Young Drago. Find. Your. Ground."
That same stoic voice spoke.

That voice broke me from the trance in which I was subdued within. I stopped the moment I heard it and if I had not, the path of lit candles has halted just before a ledge into this empty void. Smoke began to rise from the candles. That smoke did not continue to rise. It was pulled towards the cliff and sank into the darkness.

"The symbol. You now bear. Will hunger. For Power."
The stoic voice said patiently,
"Revenge is not sought. Glory is not won. Be the Drago. They wished you to be!"
this unfamiliar voice proclaimed.

There were no words for me to express. Even within the dream realm I was unable to muster my tongue. I just sat there and stared into the empty void. Although my understanding of anything was not keen, these words that were spoken, sang to my heart.

*Soon after the voices echo disappeared, the chanting began again, "**DRAGON'S WRATH!**"*

As those words were being chanted, I could hear a loud scraping sound emerging from the depths of the edge. Chains rattling around as this sound had become louder. It was as if there was something beyond, or within, the cliffs empty void that were now hauntingly being raised.

Shortly afterwards, there it was. The candle's light began to reveal what appeared to be a massive cage. As this cage continued to rise, it was beginning to tower over me. The same gate from a dream I have experienced, now facing directly towards me. Yet, the darkness overwhelmed what light there was to shadow what was contained.

The smoke from the candles were now wrapping themselves around every bar which surrounded this cage. Then soon finding their place against these massive gates I have seen before. This time, the ancient symbol that I have seen before, painted across the bars vividly.

As soon as this symbol became illuminated, the candles from the path in which I found myself trailing, began to douse out. While the tomb was becoming consumed again within the darkness, a massive smoke wall followed the path towards me.

I began to panic because I was not sure what all of this meant. I was not prepared to crawl towards the gates from before. The gates that the fiery eyes glared at me from. The gates that thicker, more violent smoke emitted from. So, I sat there. I accepted this to be my fate. Between what lies ahead, and what follows.

TO BE CONTINUED....

UPCOMING TITLES....

DRAGO BONEZ: ORIGINS
PART TWO
by Jeremy B. Pereyra

NYDELI:
WORLD BORN THROUGH MAGIC
by Jeremy B. Pereyra

PROJECT ELLESE
by Jeremy B. Pereyra

Made in the USA
Columbia, SC
20 February 2023

12576157R00141